"Help us," the woman rasped in a meager whisper.

Her gaze locked with his, and his pulse jolted into overdrive. The intensity of the connection—a demand on his very soul—sent a shiver through him.

"I will help." His simple words crackled with a sense of— what? Urgency? Finality? No, more than that, something sacred and binding. Rylan sucked in a breath.

The woman nodded slowly. Then her whole body shuddered. Her eyes rolled upward and the lids slammed closed.

Rylan shook himself and withdrew his hand from her limp fingers. What was that interaction all about? In his thirty-six years of life, he'd never experienced anything like it.

Frowning, his gaze darted toward the baby in the back seat. The little one stared back at him with wide, expectant brown eyes. Rylan had spotted no baby bag. No purse or cell phone lay in evidence either. Other than the human occupants, the car seemed strangely empty.

"Sorry, little guy," he murmured. "I don't have anything you're looking for, and your mama is in no shape to look after you. Let's get you both some help."

Jill Elizabeth Nelson writes what she likes to read—faith-based tales of adventure seasoned with romance. Parts of the year find her and her husband on the international mission field. Other parts find them at home in rural Minnesota, surrounded by the woods and prairie and their four grown children and young grandchildren. More about Jill and her books can be found at jillelizabethnelson.com or Facebook.com/jillelizabethnelson.author.

Books by Jill Elizabeth Nelson

Love Inspired Suspense

Visit the Author Profile page at LoveInspired.com.

SAFEGUARDING THE BABY

JILL ELIZABETH NELSON

LOVE INSPIRED SUSPENSE

INSPIRATIONAL ROMANCE

LOVE INSPIRED® SUSPENSE

INSPIRATIONAL ROMANCE

Recycling programs for this product may not exist in your area.

ISBN-13: 978-1-335-59752-6

Safeguarding the Baby

Love Inspired
22 Adelaide St. West, 41st Floor
Toronto, Ontario M5H 4E3, Canada
www.LoveInspired.com

Printed in U.S.A.

The Lord...relieveth the fatherless and widow:
but the way of the wicked he turneth upside down.
—*Psalm* 146:9

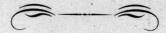

To the men and women of courage and integrity
who join with God to defend those
who cannot defend themselves and to thwart the plans
of those who prey upon the helpless.

ONE

The woman stared straight ahead, through the old car's cracked and dusty windshield. *Who* was she? *Where* was she? *Why* was she driving down an unfamiliar road in a strange vehicle? The vital questions pecked at her, but her mind returned no ready answers, only urgency and fear.

How long ago had she fled into the darkness? No telling. But now the sun rose behind her, clarifying the surroundings but lending no comfort.

The woman's gaze flicked from side to side. Barbed wire fencing hemmed her in on the right and left of the unpaved road; beyond that, dry-grass prairie sprawled in both directions as far as the eye could see. Sagebrush dotted the plain, and here and there, dark blots moved lazily across the expanse too distant to make out details. Cattle? Made sense in this environment. Far ahead, low mountains marched in ragged formation across a pale blue horizon. No human structure intruded on the wild landscape.

She—no, *they* were alone in the wilderness. A soft whimper from the back seat alerted her that the baby could awaken at any moment. *God help us!* Her heartbeat thudded in her chest. What would she do when the child woke up? She had no supplies to care for a baby. Her brow puckered. How had she come to have an infant with her but no means to meet his needs?

Like a mental snap of the fingers, a dim recollection of sudden violence played out behind the confusion that stuffed her head like a wool blanket smothering clear thought. A pair of gunmen stood over the sprawled body of a small-framed person they'd shot dead in the night. The woman had mere seconds to snatch the child in his little car seat from under the killers' noses. Then she'd run—a bullet following her...and blinding pain.

Gravel popped beneath the vehicle's tires, and the woman flinched, snapping back into the moment. Haze crowded her vision. Not from the outside—from within. She blinked hard against fading consciousness and winced as the rhythmic pounding in her head intensified. One hand lifted from the driver's wheel, and her fingers probed her left temple at the spot where the pain originated. Sticky dampness soaked the silk scarf she'd tied around the injury. Wincing, she jerked her hand away. Red fluid tinted the pads of her fingers.

Her head drooped, but she forced her neck to stiffen and brought her attention back to the road. How much longer could she cling to awareness? She needed to pull the vehicle over and stop.

No!

Stopping would be suicidal. The men would catch her—catch *them*. The men with the guns.

Her gaze darted to the rearview mirror, and a sensation like tiny ant feet skittered across her skin. A distant plume of dust marked a vehicle closing in on them. Heart in her throat, the woman's foot involuntarily mashed down on the gas pedal. The small vehicle lurched and sped up, but then the engine coughed and sputtered. The woman pumped the pedal, but no more power answered the command. The engine died, and the car began to drift to a stop.

The woman's stomach clenched. It had to be them, the killers. Who else would have followed her to this desolate area? Whatever muddled impulse had put her in this ancient sedan in the middle of nowhere, they were now isolated and at the mercy of murderers.

Breath heaving in her lungs, the woman forced her dimming gaze to focus on the dashboard. No trouble light glared at her from the instrument panel, but the reading on a single gauge told a simple story. They were out of gas.

As the car crunched to a halt at the edge of the gravel, the woman smacked the heel of her hand against the steering wheel and let out a cry. She'd failed to protect the baby. Pain ravaged her skull, and darkness ate her whole.

Sheriff Rylan Pierce narrowed his gaze as his duty SUV closed in on a rust-pocked Ford sedan stopped on the side of Wyoming's Buck County Road 7. The vehicle's dust had been pluming the air ahead of him for the past couple of miles. He'd sped up to overtake the car and discover who might be driving out this way. The Steiner's ranch headquarters was nestled at the base of the foothills, but they were gone for the next two weeks. Rylan had agreed to do periodic checks on the building site, while the neighbors were caring for the livestock.

The rickety Ford ahead wasn't one of their vehicles. No one else had any reason to be on this road.

Flicking on his lightbar, Rylan brought his vehicle to a stop behind the little sedan and then keyed up his radio. Annie Hoyt, the dispatcher at the main office in the town of Drover's Creek, answered in her usual pleasant South Carolina ex-pat drawl. Rylan had no license number to convey, since the boxy back end of the 90s Ford Taurus wore no plate, so he contented himself with updating Annie on his location and giving a description of the car. Maybe the vehicle had been reported stolen from somewhere, though why anyone would make off with the decrepit heap was beyond him. A junkyard seemed the most appropriate place for it.

Rylan's gaze searched as much of the interior of the vehicle as was visible through the rear windshield. No noticeable response to his whirling lights from anyone inside. Did the lack of movement mean the vehicle was empty? Rylan scanned his surroundings and found no fleeing figure. Not that it would have been at all smart for the vehicle's occupant or occupants to run away. There was no place to hide in the flat terrain.

Someone must still be inside, because this vehicle had been traveling until mere moments before he'd had it in sight. A short person's head could easily be hidden by the driver's-seat headrest. Still, that didn't explain why the individual had yet to make a single movement that would betray his or her presence. Rylan firmed his jaw. Best to be cautious in his approach.

With a sharp click, the door of his SUV yielded to his pressure and swung open. The early-morning promise of summer's dry heat embraced him with the pungent scent of sagebrush. A light breeze waved the dry grasses bordering the unpaved road.

Rylan placed first one booted foot and then the other onto the gravel, never letting his gaze leave the other vehicle. Still no movement from inside. Either the driver was in some sort of distress that incapacitated them or possibly the individual was armed, and they were waiting for him to show up at their window to spring an ambush. He unsnapped his handgun holster but did not draw the weapon, then stepped slowly toward the rusty car.

Still no movement visible from the Ford, but a sound began carrying to his ears. A baby fussing. Rylan's heart lurched, and his steps quickened, crunching across the gravel. He came level with the rear driver's-side window. Sure enough. A baby seat held an infant dressed in a blue onesie. His mouth puckered in a howl as his little fists pummeled the air and plump legs kicked. Rylan estimated the child's age as five or six months, though he was hardly an expert on kids. His wife's abrupt death half a decade ago—his utter helplessness to save her—had put a period on his hopes for a family.

Rylan ignored the too-familiar sensation like a knife twisting in his gut as he moved on toward the driver's window. A petite female dressed in dark green capris and a short-sleeved floral-print blouse slumped behind the wheel. The clothing seemed high-end, though he was no fashion expert, which was an incongruence with the rattle-trap car, as was the rest of her appearance. The woman's well-manicured hands, empty of weaponry, had fallen open into her lap. No ring designated her as married, but the lack of a wedding band was not definitive as to relationship status. He'd estimate her age at early to midthirties, slightly younger than himself. A red-and-yellow scarf was wrapped around the woman's head, obscuring an abundance of shoulder-length auburn hair.

No. The red on the scarf was not a natural hue of the cloth. It was...blood.

Rylan reached for the door handle. The opener button yielded, and the door creaked wide. The sharp sound elicited no response from the driver. Holding his breath, Rylan pressed two fingers to a vein in the woman's neck. Slowly, he released the oxygen from his lungs. He'd found a pulse, slow but steady.

"Ma'am? Can you hear me?"

At the words, her eyelids fluttered and then opened. Her head tilted toward him, and Rylan found himself staring into emerald-green depths. The look in her eyes shook him. Pure terror.

"You're safe, ma'am," Rylan said. "What's your name?"

A faint keening noise came from the woman's throat. Her fine-boned hand darted out and captured one of his big, rough paws in a surprisingly strong grip.

"Help us," the woman rasped in a meager whisper.

Her gaze locked with his, and his pulse jolted into overdrive. The intensity of the connection—a demand on his very soul—sent a shiver through him.

"I will help." His simple words crackled with a sense of—what? Urgency? Finality? No, more than that. Something sacred and binding. Rylan sucked in a breath.

The woman nodded slowly. Then her whole body

shuddered. Her eyes rolled upward, and the lids slammed closed.

Rylan shook himself and withdrew his hand from her limp fingers. What was *that* interaction all about? In his thirty-six years of life, he'd never experienced anything like it.

Frowning, his gaze darted toward the baby in the back seat. The little one snuffled, his tantrum slowing, and he stared back at him with wide, expectant eyes. Rylan had spotted no baby bag that would hold childcare necessities. No purse or cell phone lay in evidence, either. Other than the human occupants, the car seemed strangely empty.

"Sorry, little guy," he murmured. "I don't have anything you're looking for, and your mama is in no shape to look after you. Let's get you both some help."

Rylan strode back to his duty vehicle and got on the radio. Annie answered quickly.

"Send out the nearest ambulance," he told her. "We've got an injured female in the car. She has a head wound. Other injuries are yet to be determined."

Annie's sucked-in breath hissed through the handset. "Right away, Sheriff."

"Order a wrecker, also. The woman's vehicle is out of gas, and we'll need it towed to the shop."

Annie responded in the affirmative.

Rylan keyed the mic once more. "And have the first responders bring along baby supplies."

"'Baby supplies'?" Annie squawked back.

"The woman has an infant with her in the car, but no bag. The child appears unhurt but may need a diaper change and a feeding."

"Poor li'l tyke. You got it, Sheriff." Annie's tone had gone a bit breathless.

Rylan could hardly blame his normally unflappable dispatcher for being taken aback. The situation was beyond strange. He reaffirmed all his requests, then signed off the radio.

Lips compressed in a grim line, Rylan grabbed the first-aid kit every law enforcement vehicle in his county carried and returned to the Ford. As the baby continued to fuss, Rylan lowered the back of the driver's seat and situated the woman's upper body comfortably. Embroidery on the edge of the scarf around her head caught his attention; the black thread spelled out the letters *M* and *E*.

Did the initials provide a clue to this woman's name? He shook his head. It was too early in the investigation to reach a conclusion. Rylan gently unwound the cloth from her head. A long, angry slash of a wound across her temple became visible amid hair matted in sticky blood. His breath hitched.

Unless he was losing a step in his cop savvy, he was looking at a bullet crease. It was strange enough that he'd run across an injured woman with a baby in the middle of nowhere in a car that was barely roadworthy, but a bullet wound took the situation to a whole new level of mystery.

And danger to his safe, quiet county.

Buck County covered nearly eleven thousand square miles of Wyoming's Great Basin with a population of fewer than fifty thousand souls. Small towns of less than ten thousand dotted the map here and there among cattle and horse ranches that encompassed vast acreage.

Law enforcement was amply served by tiny municipal police departments and a county sheriff—him—with four deputies.

As he gazed at the wounded female, her features as delicate as a spring flower, scenarios for her predicament ran the gamut from an abusive spouse to some sort of gang problem to the unlikely involvement of a drug cartel. Or, perhaps, something desperately wicked that hadn't so much as entered his mind.

A prickle ran down Rylan's spine. This woman had been shot at, wounded and terrorized. She was on the run with an infant and no supplies. Should he trust the instinct whispering in his ear that she drew something big and bad in her wake?

TWO

"We're in the process of bringing Emmy out of her induced coma." A businesslike feminine voice filtered into the woman's consciousness.

"Emmy?" a deep male voice responded.

"The nurses have been calling her that because of the initials on her scarf—M. E. I have provisionally approved the designation. It's more personal than calling her Jane Doe."

The male let out a soft grunt. Acquiescence? Agreement?

"How soon do you expect *Emmy* to wake up?" he asked.

"Hard to say, but—"

"Emily-y-y." The word croaked from her dry throat as a torrent of emotions washed through her, only to disappear suddenly and with finality into an empty void in her mind.

Her eyes popped open. A white ceiling met her gaze, punctuated by a bank of fluorescent lights on dim. Even the low volume of brilliance pierced her eyeballs. She slammed her eyes shut, her head throbbing. An attempt to lift her right hand was met with modest success, but she hadn't the strength to bring it all the way to the site of her pain. The limb fell back into softness.

She must be lying in a bed. A hospital? The faint disinfectant odor permeating the air reinforced the idea. As did the soft, repetitive beeping of nearby machines. Had she been in some sort of accident? Rustles on either side of her bed betrayed people approaching.

"Is that your name?" the male asked from a point hovering above her. "Emily?"

She forced her heavy lids open to meet a steel-gray gaze embedded in a strong face of hewn planes and angles. A shiver ran through her.

"It's all right. You're safe." The man lifted a large hand, palm out. The gaze and expression softened into something approaching handsome and appealing rather than formidable and off-putting. "I'm Sheriff Rylan Pierce. Is Emily your name? What's your last name?"

"I…I don't know. Emily sounds familiar, though."

Her attention darted to the other side of the bed. A short, stocky woman wearing a white jacket and a stethoscope draped around her neck hovered just beyond the bed rail. The woman's brown-eyed gaze was gentle.

"I'm Dr. Laura Adams," she said. "Go ahead and call me Doc Laura. You sustained head trauma. You're going to be all right, but in order to allow the brain swelling to subside, you've been in an induced coma for the past five days."

"'Five days'!" The exclamation squeaked out. Her dry tongue attempted fruitlessly to moisten her lips.

"Here." The man brought a straw in a covered plastic mug to her mouth. "Why don't we go ahead and call you Emily since you recognize the name?"

With a small nod, she gave assent as she sucked greedily. Blessedly cool water flowed down her throat. He took the mug away all too soon. The tall man wore a tan-and-brown uniform with a silver badge adorning the left breast pocket. Muscular, sun-browned arms stuck out from the short sleeves of his uniform shirt, which featured the words *Buck County Sheriff's Office*, along with an insignia, on the shoulder. Where was Buck County?

Emily wrinkled her brow. "Where am I?"

"This is the Drover's Creek Municipal Hospital," the doctor answered. "Western Wyoming, dear."

The sheriff nodded. "Do you remember driving into this area of the state?"

Emily started to shake her head, but pain quelled the too-ambitious movement. "I remember driving, not knowing where I was going or where I came from. And I remember..." She drew in a sharp breath. "The baby!" The doctor's hand on her shoulder discouraged a weak lunge toward a sitting position. Emily's gaze darted wildly around the room. "Where's the baby?"

"Your son is fine, ma'am," the sheriff said.

"He's being looked after in the hospital nursery, pending foster care until you're able to resume responsibility," Doc Laura put in. "The nurses are gaga over the little guy." She smiled. "Me too."

"Do you remember *his* name?" the sheriff asked.

"No." The word came out of Emily's mouth as a faint puff of breath.

What kind of mother couldn't remember her son's

name? Or *was* the child even her son? She couldn't remember that, either. Except... Yes, she *had* given birth not long ago. But the vague knowledge lay shrouded in a blanket of pain and sorrow. How did that make sense? And why did she still feel like the child in the nursery was not her own? But if he wasn't her son, what was she doing with him? A pair of tears squeezed out the corners of her eyes and made warm tracks down the edges of her face.

"Take it easy." The doctor's gentle but firm hand remained on her shoulder. "Memory issues are not uncommon with the type of head injury you've sustained. Total amnesia is less common, but it's too early in your recovery to worry unduly. Usually at least some memory returns over time. The more you relax and don't push yourself, the more likely you'll begin to recall."

Emily's heart rate ramped up. The doc had made no promise she'd remember everything. She hadn't even guaranteed Emily would remember *anything*. What would she do if she never knew who she was?

"You don't know who shot you?" The sheriff's tone carried an edge and yanked Emily out of her *what if* dread into a new level of anxiety.

"I was shot?" Emily's jaw went slack for several heartbeats. "I assumed I must have been in an accident in order to land in the hospital."

Sheriff Pierce shook his head. "You drove out into the middle of nowhere and ran out of gas. You'd been shot sometime prior to that."

"Enough probing, Rylan." The doctor scowled at the man in uniform. "Give Emily a chance to rest and recover."

A pair of lines bracketed the lawman's mouth as he frowned, but he gave a sharp nod.

Emily's frown echoed the sheriff's. Her gut churned. If the sheriff thought *he* was frustrated at the lack of answers, he should try having his whole life swallowed by a black abyss. The bitter thought never left her lips. She was too tired to utter the words.

"Shoo, now." Doc Laura made a waving motion. "I need to examine my patient."

The sheriff lifted his hands in surrender. "Let me know if any memories begin to surface." He headed for the door.

The doctor nodded. "Count on it."

Emily didn't bother to respond. The man had annoyed and intimidated her in equal measure, but she wasn't about to make him aware of either reaction. She hauled in a deep breath. His departure had left behind a faint trace of leather-and-spice scent, almost as attractive as his dark-haired good looks. The sheriff's tanned face and the faint squint lines edging his intense eyes betrayed someone who spent a significant amount of time outdoors. His linebacker build suggested an affinity for strenuous exercise. Rugged and outdoorsy. Not her type.

Then why did her gaze linger on the doorway through which he'd disappeared? And how did she know what type she favored if she had no memory of her past?

A soft click from the other side of the bed drew Emily's attention. The doctor was holding a small penlight and smirking at her patient with a twinkle in her brown eyes. Had Emily's sense of unwelcome attraction to the sheriff shown on her face?

"That's our sheriff, all right," the doctor said. "Good man, but not big on subtlety or small talk."

"I noticed," Emily murmured.

"Now, let's check you out." The doctor shone her light into one of Emily's eyes and then the other. The woman let out a little hum, and the corners of her lips tilted upward.

"Pupils equal and reactive?" Emily's question emerged without conscious thought.

Doc Laura drew back. "You know medical terminology?"

Emily shrugged and winced at a sharp stab in her head. "Possibly I enjoy medical TV shows."

The physician chuckled. "You and millions of other people, but the shows aren't always accurate." She frowned. "How's your pain?"

"If I move too fast, a seven or eight on the pain scale—but otherwise tolerable, below five."

"More unsolicited medical jargon." Doc Laura let out a brief hum. "What you describe is within normal expectations for an injury such as yours. We'll just have to keep current on your pain meds."

Emily's thoughts churned as the doctor took her pulse and listened to her heart with the stethoscope. Was it possible she'd had some sort of medical training, or was her familiarity with such terminology misleading?

"Looking good." Doc Laura straightened and looped her stethoscope around her neck once more. "Your vital signs are stable, and your concussion seems to have eased significantly. You're going to need to take things easy over the next few weeks, but I believe you're on the mend."

"Weeks?" Emily's heart rate sped up. "I don't have that kind of time to lie around. They're coming."

"Who's coming?" The older woman's brow furrowed.

"The men."

"What men?"

"The two men who killed the woman."

"What woman?" The doctor's nostrils flared, and her eyes went wide.

"I...I don't know."

A knot formed in Emily's throat. What was the matter with her? Why couldn't she remember something so vital?

"Never mind, dear." That gentle hand came to rest on her shoulder again. "I'll pass on to the sheriff what you just told me. I'm sure he'll show up to talk to you at some point, but rest up in the meantime. Things might come back to you if you give your brain a chance to reboot. You're safe here."

Was she safe? Emily swallowed hard. Maybe. After all, the doc said she'd been lying here for five days, and nothing had happened to her. And the baby was all right.

"I want to see my..." No, she stopped the words on the tip of her tongue. *My baby* still didn't seem right. "The baby."

"We'll make that happen soon." Doctor Laura smiled down at her. "Are you hungry?"

"No." Emily's hand went to her stomach. A hollow gurgle answered the pressure. "I mean, yes. I think I could eat something."

The doctor nodded, stepping away from the bed. "I'll ask the nurse to send you in something light. Broth and crackers, perhaps? Some flavored gelatin, maybe?"

Emily nodded. "Anything."

Doc Laura turned at the doorway and regarded her. "Once you've eaten as much as you can tolerate, we'll get you up and moving around. Perhaps walk down to the nursery and see little Oliver."

"Oliver?"

The doctor laughed, a light, pleasant sound. "In lieu of good information, we named him, too. He's got the cutest little ripe olive–shaped birthmark on his plump tummy."

Emily dredged up a smile. "I guess Oliver's a fine name, then."

With a nod, the doc left, and the door swished shut behind her. Sighing long and deeply, Emily allowed her heavy eyelids to close. She'd rest for a few minutes until the food arrived. The soft blackness of sleep beckoned.

Then the nearly soundless swish of the door jerked her back from the brink of oblivion. The food already? Emily dragged her eyelids open.

An enormous dark figure rushed toward her. Emily opened her mouth to scream, and the man pounced.

Rylan strode up the hallway in the direction of Emily's room. Good thing he'd still been in the hospital parking lot, checking in with the dispatcher and his deputies, when Doc Laura called to say Emily remembered two men with guns had been chasing her. And what was this about a dead woman? That sort of serious business he needed to know more about right away. Maybe the auburn-haired mystery woman would remember additional details by the time he arrived back at her bedside.

A muffled scream wafted from the woman's room,

and Rylan's pulse rate surged as he broke into a run. Where was everyone? Not a soul sat at the nurses' station, and no one moved along the hallway. The staff must be in with patients.

He burst into Emily's room without bothering to knock. A giant of a man in a black suit—thick shoulders straining at the seams of the jacket—leaned over the woman in the bed. He was pressing a pillow into her face. Emily thrashed and clawed valiantly at the arms holding the pillow but to little effect. As Rylan took in the scene, her resistance faded.

"Stop!" Rylan bellowed.

Without removing the pillow from Emily's face, the man's attention jerked toward the interruption. Inky eyes set in a cinder block face glared at Rylan, and a snarl pulled thick lips away from yellowed teeth.

Rylan had to get that pillow off Emily's face immediately. He charged, body-slamming the man-mountain into the wall. The intruder's hot breath gushed out into Rylan's ear. Huge bear arms encircled him and began to squeeze like a boa constrictor, lifting him right off his feet. Instantly, Rylan lost the ability to take a breath. With his arms trapped against his own body, drawing his weapon wasn't possible. He kicked out, but his foot met air. He attempted to knee the man but encountered a thigh like a beam of timber. He slammed his head toward the assailant's face, but his forehead came up short against a chin like a hunk of granite. Spots danced in front of Rylan's eyes, and his ribs and spine creaked.

From the nearby bed came an outcry. A plastic projectile flew through the air and smacked into the side of the man-mountain's head. The object burst open, and water splashed out, cool droplets peppering Rylan's face. At the sudden strangeness of Emily's desperate but brilliant attack with her water container, the man's grip on Rylan loosened. He wrenched himself free. Leaping backward, his hand streaked for his duty weapon as he sucked precious oxygen into his lungs.

The assailant kicked out with startling speed. Rylan twisted to avoid a foot to the gut and took the blow on his hip. Pain spiked through Rylan's side as the strike staggered him and knocked his hand away from his gun. But he took advantage of the pivot to send his left fist toward the attacker's face. The man ducked his head quickly enough to receive the blow on his forehead rather than his vulnerable nose.

A sharp crack and a bright burst of agony told Rylan his fist hadn't fared well, but at least he'd staggered the attempted murderer. Taking advantage of the assailant's lost balance, Rylan hooked a kick at the man's knee. No matter the size of an adversary, joints were vulnerable, and this man's sheer bulk would compound an injury to the leg. A deep bellow said the man's knee had fared similarly to Rylan's hand: not well. The combatants were now 1:1 in the injury department, but an even exchange wasn't good enough. Rylan needed to get this guy under control and cuffed right now.

As he began to pull his weapon from its holster, his adversary reached under his jacket and went for a tell-tale bulk under his arm. A gun? This was the west but not the Wild West. Drawdowns were a thing of the past, weren't they? But here he was in the middle of one, a heartbeat from finding out who was the fastest.

Then a whoosh of air from the door and a startled

cry distracted them both. Quick as a striking rattler, the man lunged past Rylan and grabbed the stocky gray-haired nurse who had entered the room, bearing a tray of food. The tray and the food went flying. Whirling, the assailant flung the nurse Rylan knew as Gwen straight into him. Rylan staggered and caught Gwen as the would-be killer bulled out the door, a limp from his injured knee slowing him only slightly.

As Rylan struggled to remain upright, his feet met wetness on the floor, and he lost the battle with his balance. He landed in a heap on the tile but managed to protect Gwen from the brunt of the fall. Setting the incoherently stammering nurse to the side, Rylan heaved to his feet.

His attention darted to the patient in the bed. Emily was sitting bolt upright. Her wide, stricken gaze locked with his.

"Are you okay?" He reached out a hand but didn't quite touch her.

"Y-yes." Her word emerged in a tight hiss as she blinked against tears streaking her cheeks. "He's getting away."

Gutsy lady. She'd nearly been smothered to death, but her head was still in the game.

"Not for long." Rylan jerked a nod at her, turned and tore out the door into the hallway, his weapon finally making its way into his hand.

The hallway had been empty minutes ago, but now people scurried in his direction—a nurse, an aide and Doc Laura. Their gazes were wide as they shot questions toward him. The man-mountain was nowhere in view.

"Which way did he go?" Rylan asked, his question overriding the chorus of theirs.

The aide pointed toward the end of the hallway. "A big dude was heading for the stairway just around the corner."

Rylan spared a quick glance at the alarmed group as he trotted past them. "Take care of Emily. There's been an attempt on her life. Call for backup, lock down this hospital and set a guard at Emily's door."

"Consider it done," the doc answered smartly.

"This guy is armed and dangerous," Rylan called over his shoulder. "No one should approach him. Spread the word."

He reached the bend in the corridor, stopped and put his back to the wall, his pistol clutched in a two-handed grip. His left hand throbbed, but adrenaline suppressed the pain. Mouth dry, gut clenched, Rylan darted a glance around the corner. The stairwell door was just drifting shut.

On soft, swift feet, Rylan hurried to the door and pressed an ear to the metal. Retreating footsteps pounded the stairs, but the trajectory seemed to be upward, not down toward the street exit. The guy was headed to the third floor. How did he expect to get away? Make a break for the elevator on the upper level and head back downstairs? The route seemed needlessly convoluted, particularly when it allowed time for more law enforcement to arrive.

Rylan eased through the door and into the stairwell. Not a good situation for a firefight. Ricochets would be as dangerous as aimed bullets.

Shoving the thought to the back of his brain, Rylan

headed upward with stealthy haste. He came in view of the third-floor access door, but the footfalls continued climbing above him. Rylan's brow knotted. Was the guy going for the rooftop? With the pursuit beginning on the second floor of the hospital but with only three floors in its entirety, the big thug didn't have far to go to come out on the flat roof. At least he'd be trapped there, and Rylan should be able to hold him at bay until backup arrived. Maybe the guy would surrender before then. But from the fight the man-mountain had put up so far, easy surrender might be wishful thinking.

Breathing deeply in measured inhales and exhales, Rylan continued up the gray-painted cement steps. A sharp *kathunk* not far above betrayed a door exit bar being rammed. Hot outdoor air funneled down the stairwell, carrying with it a rhythmic roar that raised the hairs on the back of Rylan's neck. He surged up the stairs and reached the exit. Crouching low, gun at the ready, his shoulder level with the exit bar, Rylan pressed the door open.

Bullets pelted the metal door frame, a few zipping above him, where his head would have been, and smacking into the wall behind him. Rylan ducked back inside.

His gut churned. Those were no pistol shots. Someone out there had a fully automatic rifle. Not something the man-mountain could have hidden under his jacket. The guy was not alone in this attack.

Outside, the tempo and intensity of the rhythmic roar increased. Gritting his teeth, Rylan shoved the door wide but stayed back and to one side of the stairwell. The automatic-weapon assault was not repeated. Rylan risked a glance outside and spotted a small helicopter lifting off from the hospital's flat roof, which was not intended as a heliport but had served the bad guys well enough.

Rylan popped off several shots that had no effect as the bird whizzed away into the blue. Tension ebbed from Rylan's muscles as he lowered his weapon. Bitterness coated his tongue. In a road chase, he and his people would have had the upper hand in apprehending the suspects, but the county had no chopper to send after these lowlifes. For today, the suspects were gone.

But would they be back again, targeting Emily? What was going on with this woman who had no identity? Who could possibly be after her that possessed the resources for helicopter insertion and extraction, employed people with both physical bulk and lethal skills, and had access to full-auto assault weapons?

Rylan didn't have answers to those questions. Not yet. But one thing he did know: if those dangerous thugs returned, he and his people needed to be ready for anything.

THREE

"All clear," announced a masculine voice as a serious-looking man with grizzled hair and a salt-and-pepper mustache poked his torso inside Emily's room. The man wore a dark green uniform shirt, which lent him a level of officiality without being a law officer. Probably hospital security.

Something like warm wax seemed to pour through Emily's tense muscles, and she slumped against the bed's mattress, which had been elevated to a sitting position. Up until this moment, Emily had sat frozen, drawing sweet gulps of air into her lungs while staring at the door, through which her monstrous assailant and the sheriff who'd saved her had disappeared.

"Thanks, Al," said the nurse whose name tag dubbed her Gwen from where she stood at Emily's bedside.

The man nodded and withdrew from the room.

"One of our security guards." Gwen flickered a smile toward Emily, though fear still shadowed the woman's eyes.

Emily's heart rate had barely slowed in the eternal minutes since the attack, and it had taken an extra jump when distant gunshots rang out a short time ago. Now the crisis was deemed over, and her brain began to process the events. What had she been thinking, hurling that plastic container of water at the thug who'd tried to suffocate her? Though, to be fair to herself, it *had* been the only object on hand. Plus, to her amazement, the ridiculous ploy had worked.

But what about the sheriff? Had he been involved in the exchange of gunfire?

"He's all right, isn't he?" Emily managed to murmur, her throat muscles just now loosening around her vocal cords.

"Who? Sheriff Rylan? I'd be shocked if he wasn't." A strained smile formed on Gwen's face. "That guy's tougher than boot leather. Are *you* okay?"

"By the grace of God and the hard-charging sheriff, I am. Are you?"

Gwen let out a quivery laugh. "Same here. Who *was* that Frankenstein dude?" The nurse stared over her shoulder toward the door as if dreading a reappearance.

"I have no idea." Emily shuddered.

Doc Laura hustled through the door and skidded to a halt, barely managing to avoid stepping in the mess on the floor that used to be Emily's lunch. "Is everyone all right in here?"

Emily managed a shaky smile. "That seems to be the question of the day, and thankfully, the answer appears to be yes." Then a thought snagged the breath in her throat. "What about Oliver? Has anyone checked on him?"

The faces of both doctor and nurse washed white.

Emily threw the covers off her legs and started to get off the bed.

"Wait!" Doc Laura cried.

"I'm going." Emily stuck out her chin and stood upright.

Her brain swirled a bit, then settled as the chill of the floor tiles on the bottoms of her feet acted as a sensory anchor. Somewhere at the back of her consciousness, pain registered, but adrenaline had muted the ache.

Doc Laura nodded toward Gwen, who detached the IV line from the port in her hand while the doctor retrieved a thin terry-cloth robe from a nearby cabinet, as well as a pair of slipper socks. The nurse helped Emily pull the robe over her hospital gown and the socks on her feet while the doctor called out to an aide and asked him to see to cleaning up the mess on the floor. Soon— but not soon enough for Emily—Doc Laura led the way out of the room.

Urgency gripped Emily's heart. If someone had been sent to do away with her, would they also be after Baby Oliver?

The trek up the hallway and down in the elevator took forever. They were going against the flow, as staff was checking on patients after the lockdown. Finally, Emily and the others stepped onto the floor containing the nursery.

"Quick!" Emily increased her pace to a lope that overtook Doc Laura as the woman stopped in front of a broad picture window.

Oxygen vacated Emily's lungs as she stared into the nursery. To one side of the small area, a newborn lay peacefully sleeping. Definitely not Oliver. Too young, and the pink cap on the tiny head declared the child was a girl. On the other side of the room, a small crib lay on its side—empty.

"They've taken him!" Emily squeaked out.

"Taken who?" a sweet voice asked as a happy baby gurgle overlayed the question.

Emily turned, and her heart began to beat normally again. A petite nurse approached with a cooing Oliver in her arms.

"Thank You, Jesus!" Emily clutched her hands to her chest. "I've never been more scared in my life."

Oddly enough, though she had no memories of her past, she didn't doubt the statement was true. Well, almost true. Someone had just tried to kill her, and something else had happened in her recent past—the incident that had landed her and Oliver here in this hospital. These incidents ran neck and neck with the terror fading from her limbs at this moment. If only she could remember, she might know whom she feared and why they were after her and the baby.

"Where were you and Oliver?" Doc Laura demanded firmly but not harshly.

Nurse and baby stopped in front of them. This one's name tag read Julie.

Julie smiled and tickled the baby under his pudgy chin. "It was my break, so me and Little Bit took a walk outside. He's not a newborn and needs more stimulus than laying around in a crib all day. I left word at the front desk of what I was doing."

"I guess that's reasonable," the doctor said. "And your unorthodox outing averted a potential tragedy."

Emily's airway constricted. *An abduction or worse.* She didn't voice the fear.

"Thank you for looking out after Oliver." She reached for the baby, and the nurse gave him up. The infant filled her arms, and his little hands went straight for her thick hair, which was no doubt a complete rat's nest at this point. A baby tugging at it couldn't make the tangles any worse.

Nurse Julie gazed at them with her brow puckered. "Is Oliver his real name?"

"It is for now." Emily grinned at the child, and he blew bubbles at her in return.

"Is everyone all right?" The masculine tone asking the perennial question drew everyone's focus.

Sheriff Rylan strode toward them.

Emily exchanged glances with the others and let out a tense chuckle. "The better question might be, are *you* okay? We heard gunshots."

"Gunfire was exchanged, but no one was hit."

"Thank You, God," Nurse Gwen murmured.

"Your hand is swollen," Emily said, a vision of the sheriff hammering a punch toward her assailant passing before her mind's eye. Her head throbbed with the memory.

The man glanced at the member and shrugged. "I could use some ice, maybe."

"Nonsense," the doctor said. "That hand needs to be x-rayed."

"Later." The sheriff's focus never left Emily, his dark gaze cool and opaque. "It's more important that I have a chat with your patient."

Emily's face heated. Clearly this guy thought she was hiding something. Did he believe she was feigning the lost memories?

"I take it you didn't catch the guy who attacked me."

The sheriff's whole face hardened. "He must have entered the hospital in the usual way, but he escaped in a most creative manner—flying from the roof in a helicopter."

Emily joined the group—except for Oliver—in gaping at the sheriff. She swallowed against a sudden obstruction in her throat. Resources beyond anything she could have imagined were being marshaled against her and little Oliver. What was going on?

"What's going on?" asked a new masculine voice, in an echo of her thought.

Emily's gaze darted toward a large figure bearing down on them. Her skin prickled and her heart performed a little jig, but then her pulse rate settled. This guy was as big as the man who'd attacked her, but he wasn't a walking obelisk of stone with evil eyes. In fact, he was a bit soft around the edges, though his gaze was piercing, like a tough-guy teddy bear, and instead of a suit, the man wore a uniform—just not a sheriff's uniform or that of a security guard.

Sheriff Rylan turned toward the voice. "Big Dave. Glad you're on duty today."

"Always when there's an attack in my town." The guy's chin went as taut as his tone. "Fill me in."

"I'll be briefing everyone shortly." The sheriff swiveled toward Emily. "This is Big Dave Ramstead. He's the police chief here in Drover's Creek." The sheriff gestured toward the chief. "Dave, this is the woman we've spoken about. Thus far, we've tentatively identified her as Emily. No surname as of yet."

"Pleased to meet you, Emily." Big Dave inclined his head, his shrewd blue eyes assessing her.

"Likewise, Chief Ramstead." Emily mirrored the chief's demeanor with a cordial head dip accompanied by an assessing gaze.

The chief turned his attention toward Sheriff Rylan. "My people and yours are scouring the facility and grounds for further threats. I'll wait for the briefing about the specifics of the attack. Is there anything else my people can do right now?"

"Would you be able to set up a guard rotation at Emily's door? I'll lend you one of my deputies to help out."

"Can do."

Emily held up a hand. "Someone will have to guard Baby Oliver, as well. Whoever came after me was looking for him, too." She gestured toward the toppled crib in the nursery. "If Nurse Julie hadn't taken the little guy outside for a bit of fresh air, well…" She let her voice trail away, leaving the awful consequences to everyone's imagination.

The sheriff's expression turned fierce as a bird of prey, and a thrill went through Emily. That hawklike threat boded ill for the people who endangered her and Oliver. If he hadn't been on hand to stop her attacker today… Suppressing a shudder, Emily let that thought trail away, also.

"I have a solution to maximize the efficient use of personnel," the doctor said. "Now that Emily's on the mend, we could transfer Oliver's crib to her room, and you can guard them both in the same place."

Big Dave jerked a nod. "Good idea. And I'll get

someone on scouring any security camera footage for record of the intrusion."

"Thanks, Dave," the sheriff said.

Doc Laura gestured toward the elevator. "Let's get these two back to bed right now."

"I think this little guy's already gone to sleep." Emily rubbed her cheek against the soft down of Oliver's head where it rested on her shoulder.

The child let out a little snuffle as his bow of a mouth reflexively suckled the tip of the thumb between his lips.

"Let me take him and put him in a fresh crib." Nurse Julie retrieved the baby. "I'll wheel him up right behind you."

Emily's arms felt oddly empty without the child in them, but the nurse had the right idea. The throb in her head was growing stronger, and her knees were going weaker. Returning to bed sounded about right.

Minutes later, Emily reclined against the soft mattress, her head and torso raised to a half-sitting position. The floor had been mopped up sometime while they were out of the room. As Nurse Julie situated Oliver in his crib against the wall, Sheriff Rylan took a seat at Emily's bedside. The man's steel-gray gaze fixed on her, though he didn't say a word. The nurse rustled out of the room, and the sheriff sat forward.

"Thank you," Emily said softly, forestalling the first question. "You saved my life."

A strange expression flitted across the sheriff's face. Pain, yes. And grief tinged with guilt? Why would that be?

"You're welcome," he said with a smile that could easily have been confused with a grimace.

Her gratitude had made the sheriff uncomfortable. An overdeveloped sense of modesty? No, the barely concealed emotion was far stronger than that. Comprehension jolted her insides. This man had lost someone close to him that he hadn't been able to save like he'd saved Emily. Her heart tore for him...and for herself.

Why did she think she'd experienced loss like the sheriff's? Had there been someone she'd failed to save?

Emily's head went light, as if it had become filled with helium. Whatever tragedy had occurred took place before the danger that swirled around her now. How did she know that? If only she could remember. But did she truly *want* to recall?

Rylan studied the furrows that suddenly rippled Emily's brow, and his gut tightened. "Do you remember something?"

Her forehead smoothed, and she shook her head. "Only that there's something I *don't* want to remember. Something from before I ended up on the run."

Rylan frowned. "Is the thing before connected with the danger now?"

He waited as she took several long breaths.

"I don't think so," she answered at last with a shake of her head.

He sighed. More vagueness.

"I'm frustrated, too," she snapped.

"Of course you are. I can't even imagine. But I don't know whom I'm protecting you from or why. Lack of information makes the situation exponentially more difficult."

"What are we going to do?"

Tension ebbed from Rylan's shoulders, and he let out a brief chuckle. "I'm glad you said *we*, Emily. For whatever protection detail my office figures out, your full cooperation and engagement will be the best help."

"You've got it."

"Good." Rylan nodded. "You've proved your courage and ingenuity. Thank you, by the way, for your creative touchdown pass on that goon's head with your plastic water mug. I was running out of oxygen." He offered her a lopsided grin.

She answered with a blush and a brilliant smile. Reflexively, Rylan lowered his gaze. He didn't have time for the cartwheels his heart performed when those green eyes sparkled at him. A soft knock came at the door, saving him from further discomfort.

"Who is it?" Rylan's hand moved toward his weapon. It was absurd to think that someone who was a threat would knock, but he couldn't be too careful.

"Nurse Gwen," a gentle voice answered.

"Come in," Emily said.

The nurse eased softly through the door, her gaze on the crib, where the baby lay napping. Gwen carried a fresh tray of food.

"Are you still hungry?" the nurse asked, shifting her attention to Emily.

"I am," her patient answered.

"It will be good for you to take some nourishment." Gwen moved toward the bed. "And then you need to rest." She stared sternly at Rylan.

"I can tell when I'm not welcome." He started to rise, but Emily reached out a hand and gripped his wrist. The touch warmed him from top to toe.

"Please stay while I eat," she said. "I need you to fill me in on whatever your investigation has uncovered. I mean, I assume you've been busy looking into what's going on with me and Oliver in the five days I've been asleep."

Rylan frowned and settled again into his chair, but he held off on speaking. His gaze followed Gwen as she placed the food tray on Emily's overbed table and swiveled it until the flat top sat in front of her patient's torso. With the touch of a button, Emily raised the head of her bed farther and then removed the lid from her plate, revealing a steaming bowl of broth. A meaty aroma filled the room. She picked up her spoon as Gwen turned toward Rylan.

"Radiology is waiting on the first floor to x-ray that hand," the nurse said.

"I'll be there shortly," he answered, keeping the injured member out of sight below the bed. His left hand *was* throbbing and, last time he'd looked, had gone as puffy as a catcher's mitt.

"No weaseling out of a thorough examination." Gwen wagged a finger at him.

Rylan grimaced. "You got it."

Emily chuckled. "Apparently, the medical staff are aware of certain tendencies you have, Sheriff Rylan."

Gwen sniffed. "He forgets about his own needs when he's caught up in serving the people of his county. We're grateful for his dedication, but I'm old enough to be his mama, so I'm going to mother him a bit."

Rylan's face heated, but his mouth relaxed into a grin. "Thanks, Gwen. I think."

The nurse delivered a satisfied nod and rustled out of the room.

"She's a gem," Emily said. "Now, to business. What can you tell me?"

"We fingerprinted you."

Her spoon paused halfway to her mouth as her lips formed a slight frown. "I don't like it, but that's actually a reasonable thing to do." She shrugged and took the bite of broth.

"Your prints are not in any database, criminal or otherwise," Rylan said.

"That's a good thing for my character but not helpful in identifying me."

The sheriff frowned. "It's an interesting result since Doc Laura told me you seem familiar with medical terminology. But if you were a health-care worker, your fingerprints would be in the system."

"I guess that eliminates one type of occupation, with thousands remaining."

Rylan jerked a nod. "We checked into missing person's reports for a five-state area, but any missing female that vaguely resembled you turned out not to be you once we matched photographs. Same for Baby Oliver. So, apparently, no one has reported you or Oliver missing."

Emily frowned but said nothing as she continued eating. She'd moved on to the small cup of green gelatin.

"You were carrying no identifying documents on your person," Rylan continued, "and a search of the vehicle you drove produced no purse, no wallet, no anything identifying you or the baby. In fact, the car was empty of belongings. Even the glove compartment was bare."

"That's weird." Emily set her spoon and gelatin cup down.

"We did discover an explanation for that oddity when we traced the vehicle's VIN number. The Taurus belonged to a man from Burling, a town the next county over, a good hundred miles away. By arrangement with the business owner, he'd dropped the car off after hours at a scrap yard the evening it went missing. He cleaned everything out of the vehicle and slipped the title through the mail slot at the yard's business office but left the vehicle's keys in the ignition. Nobody considered for a second that someone would make off with the hunk of junk."

Emily paled and gaped at him. "I *stole* a car?"

"It would seem so, but no one's out to press charges." Rylan offered her a smile. "The vehicle was all but worthless, and it would appear the circumstances were extreme. Someone shot you, and you were fleeing."

"Nobody in Burling knows me, then? I'm not from there?"

"Burling isn't your place of residence, but you *were* seen."

"I was? By whom?"

"The scrap yard where you acquired the Taurus is only a block behind the Western Lodge. The clerk at the hotel remembers you checking in."

Emily gasped and sat up, stiff. "Surely the hotel has a record of who I am."

Rylan shook his head. "This is where it gets really weird. The clerk remembered you when we showed him your picture, but he didn't recall your name. When he tried to access the records from that night on his computer, they had been wiped. No trace at all of anyone checking in or out. Just gone."

Emily gave a little shiver. "We've already seen that these people who are after me possess extraordinary resources."

Rylan's gut clenched. *Exactly.* That fact occupied a high place on his worry list.

"There's more," he said. "The clerk did remember what room he gave you, but it had been cleaned and re-rented since then. A conversation with the housekeeper who serviced the room the morning after your check-in said it was strange, but when she went into the room the morning after you left, it almost looked like no one had ever stayed there. And further, whatever vehicle you arrived in—not that nasty sedan you took under fire—was missing from the lot. There were no unaccounted-for vehicles. Someone thoroughly cleaned up after you. Attempted to erase your presence."

A sheen of tears washed across Emily's eyes, and her lips trembled. "What about the dead woman I saw? And the gunmen?"

"The shooters are undeniably real. You have the wound to prove it—and the circumstantial evidence of a follow-up attack by an armed intruder in this very hospital. However, there were no murders reported in or around Burling in the time frame."

"No dead body?"

Rylan shook his head.

"What about Oliver? Is he mine or the murdered woman's child?"

"He could well be yours. Doc Laura's initial examination when you were brought in determined you'd given birth by cesarean section sometime in the past year." An expression of deep pain flitted across Emily's face, then suddenly disappeared. Rylan bit his tongue against questioning the reaction. If her memory loss was a pretense, his next words might elicit a telling response. "The odd thing is, the doc feels, by the amount of healing on the scar, that the incision was made nine to twelve months ago—not less than six months ago, which would match Oliver's age."

Emily opened her mouth, a distant expression in her eyes, and then pressed her lips together with a shake of the head. "I have no explanation for that. Maybe I heal quickly."

Rylan released an acknowledging grunt. "A DNA test would answer the question if he's yours or not."

She jerked a nod. "Let's do it."

No hesitation in the acquiescence. Was he glad she didn't seem to be deliberately hiding something, or was he disappointed that her amnesia kept him from vital answers about the current situation?

Emily's expression firmed, then abruptly shattered as a sob shook her chest and the tears came. Instinctively, Rylan took her hand, and she squeezed it hard enough to grind his knuckles together. He might need X-rays on both hands, but he wasn't about to pull away.

The door opened, altering the air pressure in the room. Rylan looked over his shoulder. Doc Laura approached, eyebrows drawn together, focus on her patient. Still weeping, Emily rolled onto her side and pulled herself into a huddle under the sheets.

"Let her calm down and rest," the doc murmured.

With a nod, Rylan got up and left the room. An invisible band constricted his diaphragm. He couldn't imagine the torment of not knowing who you were or why you were being hunted by murderous thugs backed by someone with incredibly deep and sinister capabilities. He *had* to figure it out…and fast. No way were those people going to stop attacking.

Firming his jaw, Rylan made his way down to the X-ray department. It turned out he had a cracked knuckle and a fractured finger. He accepted a cold pack for the swelling, a splint to hold things in place while his hand healed and a hefty stock of nonnarcotic painkillers. Then he checked on the protection detail outside Emily and Oliver's room, found an alert officer stationed at the door and departed the hospital without going in to speak with Emily again. Hopefully, she was sleeping. Rest was the best thing for her right now, both physically and mentally.

He arrived at the offices the county sheriff's personnel shared with the Drover's Creek Police Department to find the place buzzing with fresh efforts to track down Emily's assailants, from earlier in Burling and here in the hospital. Local airports were being contacted to see if any helicopters had taken off from there, and ranchers were being solicited for any information about a helicopter flyover of their property. With such a sparse population, though, a chopper might have passed through the area unnoticed.

"Good initiative," he told everyone, then called a meeting in the conference room.

Whoever wasn't out on patrol huddled up around the

big, scarred table that took up most of the space. Ideas for avenues of investigation were tossed around, assignments given and the rotation for protection detail at the hospital finalized.

"I want a safe house found for Emily and Oliver that can be occupied as soon as they're discharged from the hospital. Someplace out of the way but defensible."

Deputy Sarah Lawrence raised a willing hand. "I'll look into locating a property."

Rylan nodded. That was a good assignment for Sarah since she was on desk duty until she fully healed from a sprained ankle suffered in rescuing a daring young child who'd climbed too high up the side of a cliff. His chest swelled. He had some brave and selfless deputies on his team, but as the leader, he had to make sure they stayed as safe as possible while protecting the citizens and—most particularly at this moment—the dependent strangers they had welcomed into their midst.

"As soon as I find out when Emily will be released," Rylan went on, "I'll let you—"

"Tomorrow." Annie's voice came from the doorway, her infectious grin aimed at them all. "Doc Laura just called. She says Emily and Oliver will be released in the morning."

"Then we need to work fast, people." Rylan turned toward Big Dave. "Can you supply a patrol car with a couple of officers to pull up under the canopy over the hospital's front door and pretend to pick up our charges? If we're being surveilled, the unit can lead the watchers on a wild-goose chase all over town."

"You got it," the police chief answered. "I'll issue a tail car, too, as backup in case our diversion draws fire."

"Good thinking. While the fake-out is going on, I'll take my personal vehicle to an obscure entrance and make off with Emily and Oliver under the radar."

A few more ideas were batted around, the plan was fine-tuned and then the meeting broke up with everyone scattering to their assignments. Rylan left law enforcement headquarters, rolling his shoulders against residual aches and pains from his fight with Emily's assailant at the hospital. His injured hand throbbed. He'd ice it again before turning in for the night. But first, he had chores to do at home.

Rylan climbed into his crew-cab pickup and headed out of town. In less than ten minutes, he was turning into the long driveway toward his modest ranch house. In the pasture to one side of the driveway, Hank and Pearl, his quarter horses, lifted their heads and looked at him, then returned to their grazing, tails swishing against their sleek flanks. Rylan smiled. The pair might act like his arrival home meant nothing to them, but the second he rattled the feed bucket, they'd race each other to the barn for their oats and a cushy stall to sleep in overnight.

Then Rylan sobered, fighting back an old and too-familiar ache in his chest. Five years ago, the fenced pasture had been much larger, containing a thriving and growing herd of quarter horses lovingly tended by his wife while he looked out for the county as a deputy sheriff. After Sheryl's passing, Rylan hadn't been able to maintain both occupations, and he'd sold most of the horses and some of the land. He'd hung on to Hank, his favorite mount, and he hadn't been able to bring himself to part with Pearl, his wife's pride and joy.

Shaking off the melancholy, Rylan pulled the truck under the carport attached to the house and stepped out to an enthusiastic tail-wagging greeting from his Australian shepherd, Sheba. He scratched the dog behind the ears, then headed up onto the porch and into the house. A few minutes later, he emerged, changed out of his uniform into jeans and a well-worn T-shirt, to find Sheba sitting sentry at the door, ready to accompany him for evening chores.

"It's going to be short and to the point tonight, Sheba," he told the animal. "We won't be going for our evening ride. I'm bushed, and I've got a big day ahead tomorrow."

Sheba wagged her stubby tail and woofed as if she understood. The stalls were quickly mucked, and the horses fed and put up for the night. Then, after a brief round of fetch with Sheba, Rylan gobbled down a sandwich and headed for bed. But he didn't sleep. Not much, anyway.

His mind's eye kept picturing the anguish on Emily's face. Then he would envision her smile. Everything in him wanted to keep her safe. To hold her close. Why was it so hard for him to keep a professional distance from this woman?

He sat up, punched his pillow into shape and then flopped back down. Finally, he drifted into slumber… straight into the grip of a boa constrictor. Squeezing. Squeezing. He jerked awake with a gasp. Cold sweat covered his face, and his hand throbbed in time with his galloping pulse. As he sucked in long, precious breaths, he checked the bedside clock.

5 a.m.

He might as well get up. Going back to sleep didn't

seem likely with his heart still flailing against his ribs. Besides, he had some preparations to make in his vehicle and with certain personnel for the pickup at the hospital in a few hours.

Nine o'clock in the morning found him dressed in civilian clothes and drawing his late-model Chevrolet Silverado crew-cab truck to within a few feet directly outside an obscure exit from the hospital. He kept a sharp watch on the environment as a pair of deputies escorted Emily, with Oliver in her arms, out the door. All lay quiet in the parking areas, sidewalks and grassy verges within the hospital grounds. Nothing seemed out of place in the normal commerce going in and out of the restaurant across the road.

The rear passenger-side door opened, and Emily stuck her head inside. Rylan glanced back to see she was dressed in the jeans and lightweight yellow top Annie had rounded up from one of her teenage grandkids to fit Emily's petite form. A single strip of white bandaged the healing head wound. Otherwise, her hair formed a glorious auburn mane framing a lovely heart-shaped face.

Emily smiled at him, and Rylan's heart tripped over itself. *Get it together, bub*, he snarled at himself.

"I see you've got Ollie's car seat strapped in here," she said.

"A technical operation beyond me. One of my deputies who has children had to do it."

Chuckling, she situated the bright-eyed baby in the seat and clicked his oddly configured series of belts into place like a pro. Rylan lifted his eyebrows. Since Emily was so unsure about being Oliver's mother and the timeline of her cesarean and Ollie's age didn't fit, he'd started leaning toward the murder victim as the parent. *Alleged* murder victim, anyway. It was hard to call it for sure unless a body had been located. Now, Emily's expertise with this type of car seat argued in favor of *her* being the mother. Unless, of course, she'd delivered a baby a year ago that was not Oliver. But if that were the case, where was the other child? Rylan mentally shook his head. Pivotal questions, but the mystery of Emily's relationship to Oliver would soon be solved by the return of the DNA results.

"Climb in," he said. "Our decoy vehicle should be pulling out into traffic about now, hopefully drawing any surveillance away from this area."

As a deputy ushered her into the front passenger seat, Emily's expression sobered, dimming the light in her emerald gaze. "Let's do this." She buckled herself in.

Rylan put a hand on his sidearm as he directed his truck away from the hospital and onto a back-access road. They took a few turns, avoiding the main business and traffic areas, where lots of eyes could spot them. Soon they reached the outskirts of town, and habitations began to become fewer and farther between on either side of them. Several blocks ahead, open prairie sprawled. It would be tough to sneak up on anyone from that direction.

"We're nearly there," he told her. "It's that little blue house in the next block."

Rylan scanned his peripherals and then his rearview mirror. A massive black Escalade whipped around a corner two blocks back and began bearing down on them.

"Hang on." Rylan accelerated his vehicle. "We've got company behind us."

Emily gasped. "And ahead of us."

Rylan turned his gaze forward as another Escalade charged out of a side street half a block to their fore and stopped in the intersection, stalling their progress. Gritting his teeth, he braked the pickup to a halt. His rearview mirror told him the hulking SUV to their rear had halted a few yards behind them.

They were boxed in. Things were about to get interesting.

FOUR

Emily fought to take in a full breath as desperate prayers streamed through her mind. Was she a person of faith in her unremembered life? Quite possibly. The praying certainly came naturally. Then again, anyone might cry out to God in a situation like this.

Her head was on a swivel as she alternated her wide gaze between the giant vehicles enclosing them in a trap. The windows in both the Escalades were too dark to make out more than silhouettes of people filling the front and back seats, at least four per vehicle. The three of them—one an infant and another an unarmed civilian—were grossly outmatched.

"What if they start shooting?" Emily's voice emerged as a bare thread of sound.

"They haven't even rolled down their windows yet." The sheriff's head turned to gaze over his shoulder at the large SUV behind them. "Maybe they want to talk."

"Talk? Not likely, if the hospital attack was any indication."

Rylan unsnapped the weapon holster on his belt.

Emily's heart squeezed in on itself. "We can't have gunplay near the baby."

"I'll do anything I can to avoid that." The sheriff's gaze continually flitted between the threat in front of them to the rearview mirrors monitoring the threat behind them. "But I have no control over what they decide to do. I'm not about to allow them to shoot us."

Rylan commanded the Bluetooth phone hookup on his dash screen to call one of his deputies. The man answered almost immediately.

"Do you have our location?" the sheriff asked.

"We do. We're less than a block out from you."

"Initiate the deterrent protocol we discussed."

Before Emily could ask about this deterrent protocol, the rear driver's-side door of the Escalade in front of them opened. She sucked in a breath. No weapon showed yet, but a large booted foot appeared, lowering beneath the half-open door. Then the big black barrel of a shotgun poked out. Next to her, Rylan's breath hissed while hers froze in her lungs.

Suddenly, a pair of sirens let out tandem *whoop-whoops*, then ceased. A sheriff's deputy SUV rolled up to the rear bumper of the enemy vehicle ahead of them. The booted foot and the shotgun barrel withdrew, and the Escalade's door closed. Emily looked over her shoulder to see a police cruiser coming up on the Escalade behind them. The massive SUV to their rear suddenly began to move and turned smoothly into an alley while the Escalade in front of them simply glided ahead into the next block, both vehicles proceeding on a path perpendicular and away from them. The law enforcement vehicles followed, almost riding their bumpers.

Emily's pent-up breath left her in an audible gust. *Thank You, Lord.*

The sheriff growled wordlessly under his breath. "Run the plates while you stay on them," he said through the phone connection, which had remained open.

"We're on it."

"Call in backup. When it arrives, pull these jokers over. Use extreme caution. Get them to show you their firearms license and ask for identification from everyone in each vehicle. If everything's legit, you won't be able to arrest them, but you can stay on their tails. If they go somewhere in town, see where they stop and who gets out. If they leave Drover's Creek, find out where they go. If they stay on the road, escort them out of this county."

"Ten-four, with pleasure," the deputy answered.

"We'll proceed to the retreat location," the sheriff added.

"Escorts are on the way," the deputy said, and Rylan ended the call.

"'Retreat location'?" Emily stared at him as the sheriff sent their vehicle forward and turned a corner, directing them back toward the heart of town.

A city squad car whipped out of a side street in front of them and took its place in the vanguard while a second squad car moved into place behind them.

"Yes, I'll be taking you both to the station," Rylan said. "As unbelievable as it may seem, somehow the people who are after you knew where we were going. If we've lost the advantage of secretly relocating you, then the cop shop is the safest place for you, the baby and my community."

"Your community? Oh!" The larger reality of the situation hit her like a blow to the gut. "If you can't keep our location unknown to the enemy, then Oliver and I need to be someplace where a gunfight won't break out around civilians."

"Exactly." The sheriff sent her a dark glance.

"I'm so, so sorry."

Rylan's brows rose. "No need to be sorry. None of this is your fault."

"How do we know I'm not guilty of something when I can't remember what happened or anything about my life?"

The question had blurted out from her lips, a product of vague feelings of guilt that plagued her psyche whenever she was alone. Who was she? Had she done something to deserve this unease about herself? If only she had answers.

The sheriff opened his mouth, then shut it again. He gusted out a long breath. "Whatever the explanation for the deadly pursuit of you and this child, it's clear you're protecting the baby. I find no culpability there."

"Thank you." Warmth spread in her chest. "I hope if—no, *when*—my memories return, your confidence in me is confirmed."

Sourness settled on her tongue. Something awful had happened in her recent past, leaving an aftertaste of desperation and despair. Whatever it was had involved officials in some fashion. Absent specific memories, she didn't understand how she could know that tidbit, but she did. Could she be a wicked person caught up in bad deeds with bad people? Is that why her life was in danger?

"But what if I'm a kidnapper and these people are trying to get their baby back?"

Again, her racing thoughts had spurted from her lips before she could clamp her jaw shut against them. Why would she want the sheriff to suspect her of wrongdoing? Why would she suspect herself? Sure, the sheriff had claimed she had no criminal record, but not all crooks had ever been arrested. But, no, seeing herself as a kidnapper didn't feel right at all. If anything, her adversaries were the kidnappers...and murderers, too. That poor woman lying on the ground. Emily blinked away the horrible image and turned her attention to the sheriff.

Rylan tucked his chin toward his chest and raised his eyebrows as if in thought. Then he snorted a chuckle. "If there was anything legitimate about your attackers, your being in custody would be nothing but a relief for them. They would be going through proper channels to reclaim the child and see justice done, not trying to kill you under the noses of law enforcement. Besides, you remember witnessing a murder."

"I do and I don't." She shook her head. "It's beyond frustrating to have no context for the images flashing through my brain."

Rylan nodded. "Anyone would be second-guessing themselves under the circumstances." He clucked his tongue. "Here we are."

They had driven through a downtown district lined with businesses, and now they turned a corner onto a side street. Then the sheriff directed the pickup truck into a fenced-in parking lot and pulled up next to a single-story redbrick building in a spot marked with a sign reserving it for the sheriff. Their escort vehicles halted close around them. Uniformed city police exited the units and surrounded the pickup, weapons drawn and gazes scanning the area.

"You have good people working for you," Emily said.

"And *with* me, though I wonder…" Rylan's voice trailed off, and his lips turned downward.

Emily sent him a hard stare. Of course! He had to be asking himself how their plans had become known. Her mouth went dry. Did Sheriff Rylan have a traitor among his own? If so, how safe were she and Oliver, even here surrounded by law enforcement personnel who had sworn to protect and serve?

Stomach in knots, Rylan turned toward Emily. "Let's get you inside."

She nodded, her face pale.

He stepped out of the cab while officers closed in to assist Emily as she and the baby got out of the vehicle. Not content to leave Oliver in another's care, Emily quickly took the baby from the deputy who had retrieved him from his car seat. Rylan could hardly blame her for her protectiveness—another indication that she could well be the boy's mother. Plus, despite her memory issues, she was a sharp one. She must have realized—like he had—that there might be a leak in Buck County's law enforcement.

Nausea flowed through Rylan. Everything in him rebelled against the suspicion. He'd known some of those people most of his life and, until this moment, would have trusted any of them *with* his life. *Hold on, now.* Nothing had been proven. There *had* to be another explanation, and he meant to find it.

Through a side door, they entered the county sheriff's office, which doubled as a municipal police station. Rylan took up the rear and stepped inside last. The familiar odors of brewing coffee, paper and ink, and the finish that coated the vintage hardwood floors washed over him in a comforting tide. The murmur of voices and the muted *tap-tap* of keyboard typing soothed his ears. This place was his home away from home. His shoulders relaxed, but then he firmed them. There would be no letting down his guard yet.

"Get Emily and Oliver settled as comfortably as possible in my office," he told his people as they entered the square bullpen at the center of the building, where his four deputies and the six municipal police officers had their desks.

The police chief had his own office, as did Rylan, though judging by the chief's open door and lack of lighting inside, the man wasn't present. Big Dave kept his workspace spartan, with Rylan's only slightly less so thanks to the tall pile of files that sat in the corner of his desk. But at least in his office, Emily and Oliver could take advantage of an old sofa that sat against a far wall, where he sometimes slept when things were especially busy, like when the county fair was going on. Parking Emily and the baby in a desk chair wouldn't do long-term, and he had no idea when the department would feel comfortable relocating them.

Only an officer who was normally on night duty, plus a few ancillary personnel—both day and night staff—were at the desks scattered throughout the squad room. Everyone else was either patrolling or had been involved in the integrated city/county plan to stash Emily and

Oliver in a safe house. The department was all-hands-on-deck today.

With Oliver hugged tight in her arms, Emily turned toward the group—some standing and some sitting but all gazing at her. "Thank you. Everyone here and all the staff at the hospital have been so nice to Ollie and me. We're strangers, but you've treated us like one of your own. I don't know where we'd be without you."

Smiles bloomed on multiple faces as a chorus of *you're welcome*s swept the room. Emily's gaze sought Rylan's, and he responded with a nod. Despite the possibility of an unfriendly party mixed in with the present company, she'd responded graciously during a tense time and won over his people with a few words. The woman had the class to go with her unpretentious beauty. Too much class. She was out of his league, and best he remember that.

Forcing himself to turn away, he headed toward the dispatcher's station in the next room to the bullpen and near the public front door. Annie was seated behind the raised counter, its attached bulletproof glass separating her from potential visitors. As soon as he came up behind her, the pleasant-faced dumpling of a woman turned her head toward him.

"Where's Big Dave?" he asked.

"Out and about in his cruiser. Said someone had to keep an eye on the rest of the town with so many personnel involved in moving Emily and Oliver."

Rylan nodded. "Good thinking. What's the word from our units on the trail of those Escalades?"

The dispatcher frowned and shook her head. "Those lowlifes stopped, pretty as you please, when the deputies pulled them over. All their paperwork was in order—both IDs and firearms permits—so no arrests were made. No wants or warrants on any of the eight thugs, provided they were using genuine ID. And weren't they smug about it when our people had to let them go? Maddening. Right now, they're drivin' slow and steady as your granny up the highway toward the Utah border. Not strayin' a mile over the speed limit. Our units are keepin' on their tails."

Rylan snorted. "Suspiciously law-abiding."

"You got that right."

"How about the license plates?"

"They come back to a rental agency in Salt Lake City. The rental was paid for in cash in the name of a limited-liability company based in San Diego, California—Centaur Financial Group. That's as far as I've gotten in my research."

"Good progress." Rylan patted the shoulder of the woman he regarded as highly as a second mother. "Keep digging while I meet with the staff in the conference room. Once I'm done with the meeting, if you've got a phone number for the LLC, I'm going to give them a call and ask why they have a presence in Drover's Creek, Wyoming."

"I'm on it." Annie nodded and smiled as her fingers danced across her keyboard.

Rylan returned to the bullpen and told his staff to grab any updated reports and meet him in the conference room. The alacrity with which his order was obeyed in a muted cacophony of paper shuffling and footsteps betrayed the unease flowing through the entire department. Rylan gritted his teeth. How he hated playing defense in the dark. They needed some answers soon.

"Get settled, and I'll be right in," he told the small herd as they swept past him.

Rylan strode to his office and then halted at the closed door. As if this day could get any stranger, he found himself needing to knock on his own office door, but he wasn't about to barge in and startle his guests. Emily's voice bade him to enter. He stepped inside and found the woman seated on the sofa with Oliver on her lap. She was teaching him patty-cake. The happy infant giggles eased a bit of the oppressive weight from Rylan's chest.

He smiled at Emily, and she returned the gesture, though her gaze held little levity.

"Did your people arrest whoever was in those Escalades?"

Rylan shook his head. "The goon squad is retreating sedately."

"At least they're going away." Emily let out a deep sigh. "I understand your need to do things by the book, but if we aren't able to question anyone, where are we going to get the answers to what's going on?"

"We're working on it. Does the name Centaur Financial Group, LLC, mean anything to you?"

Her brow puckered as several beats of silence passed. "Sorry. I don't have the tiniest inkling of a response to that name."

"No worries, but I had to ask. Can I get you anything?"

"I'm fine. Someone brought me something to drink." She gestured toward his desk, where a bottle of water sat. "And I've got all of Oliver's things right here." She patted the diaper bag the hospital had supplied her with when they left that morning.

"Very good, but don't hesitate to sing out if you need anything. I'm going into a meeting with my people. We *will* get to the bottom of how those bozos in the SUVs knew where to find us."

Emily locked gazes with him, expression as stern as his own. "I know you will."

Rylan gave her a nod and then turned to head for the conference room, his tread lighter for her faith in him. Now he needed to restore the faith and trust in his department. He stepped into the room where his people had gathered, and every eye rested on him, sober and intense. Taking his place at the head of the table, he met each gaze, one by one, and none flinched or turned away. A pin drop would have echoed like a thunderclap.

"Thoughts about how our plans were uncovered?" Rylan modulated his tone to come out soft but deadly sober.

A hand tentatively went up, and Rylan acknowledged Deputy Sarah Lawrence with a nod. Angry color tinted Sarah's normally pale cheeks, and her face wore an uncharacteristic scowl.

"I hate to say it, but our leak had to come through the hospital personnel because it sure wasn't one of us."

A rumble of agreement went around the room.

Rylan huffed a long breath through his nose. "I can see that as a possibility concerning the clandestine exit from the hospital, though only a few of their staff members knew that much. However, no one at the hospital had an address of where we were going, and the Escalades waylaid us only a block from our destination.

That said, I can't wrap my head around anyone in this department giving out information about a case, much less endangering a woman and her baby."

"How about if the leak was involuntary?" asked Steven Gray, their IT and head evidence guy and very occasional fill-in dispatcher. In small departments such as theirs, everyone donned multiple hats as needed.

"What do you mean by 'involuntary'?" Rylan canted his head at the husky man staring at him with intense blue eyes magnified by black-rimmed glasses.

"What if someone has been listening in on conversations inside this building?"

"You mean like through some kind of electronic bug?"

"Or a parabolic microphone trained on the building."

A babble of voices erupted. Rylan made out an exclamation of *Oh, you tech dudes!* along with an eye roll from Sarah. He lifted his hand for quiet, and the scoffing subsided.

"Let's hear Steve out." He gave the man a nod. "Go on."

Steve leaned forward, resting his thick forearms on the tabletop, an eager light on his face. "I'm inclined toward suspecting the bug because we'd notice strangers hanging out nearby in a van or other vehicle so they could point the mic at a window. But people come in and out of the front office all the time."

Rylan sat back in his chair. "Are bugs that easy to plant that anyone could slip one in somewhere unnoticed?"

Steve nodded. "Sure. The tech for that sort of thing has gotten very sophisticated and very small. Some stranger walks in to make an innocuous inquiry and leaves his little gift behind. It could be that simple."

Rylan got on his cell phone and called Annie at the front desk. "How many strangers have come into the reception area in the past twenty-four hours?" he asked as soon as she answered.

Several beats of silence fell, then the woman let out a soft hum. "Just one guy that I can remember. He asked if we had any ordinances against door-to-door sales, and I said we didn't. The guy smirked like the proverbial canary-eating cat and walked out without another word. I didn't like him. He had a predatory air about him, as if he'd be a strong-arm type of sales rep. Not the sort of person we want out and about among our more vulnerable populace. I dropped a word into the community grapevine to keep an eye out for him and report any underhanded behavior. My written report of the encounter should be on your desk."

Rylan harumphed. "I haven't had a chance to look at it. Sometimes it's too bad we can't arrest people for what vibes they give off. What did he look like?"

"Short and lean, with a nose like a parrot's beak and a mouth like a pencil slash. He was wearin' one of those fedora hats and a snazzy pinstriped suit over a white shirt with no tie. I couldn't see the color of his eyes because he had sunglasses on. Why do you want to know?"

"Sit tight. Steve, Sarah and I are going to come out there and search your workstation."

Annie started to squawk like one of those parrots she'd mentioned, but Rylan cut the call.

He rose, motioning toward the pair he'd named. "With me."

Rylan's gut roiled as he left the conference room. If a bug was found, he and the entire staff would be ready to turn cartwheels because their department's integrity would be proven intact. On the other hand, if a bug turned out to be present, it would be his fault that their plans had been exposed. Though he hadn't outlined the entire plan while in the dispatch area, late yesterday afternoon he'd briefed Annie loud and clear on the safe house address. From his mouth straight into the enemy's ears.

FIVE

Something like a muted cheer carried to Emily's ears as she laid a sleeping Oliver on a blanket on the floor. She didn't dare leave him on the sofa because he was old enough to roll off. The commotion drew her to the door, and she peered out into the squad room. Not a soul sat at a desk. Everyone milled around an open doorway at the far end, delivering high fives to each other. Emily stepped out of Rylan's office and drew his door nearly shut behind her, leaving it open a crack so she could hear Oliver if he fussed.

"What's going on?"

"There's no leak in the department," a fresh-faced, young female deputy announced with a grin.

"Except there is." Rylan's sober pronouncement preceded his entrance from the outer room into the bullpen. He held up a clear plastic bag containing a thin, square black chip no more than the size of a quarter. "It's a listening device someone planted under the lip of the dispatcher's desk yesterday, indicating one more way law enforcement in this county needs to up its game." He thrust the bag toward the female officer. "Get this dusted for prints." Then he pointed toward a tall, stocky man in plain clothes. "Add *daily bug-sweep* to your job description, Steve."

"Yes, sir. Does that mean I get to order more gadgets?"

"Whatever you need to get the task done," Rylan answered. "Within reason."

The young man grinned like Christmas had come early, then trotted toward a desk in the far corner that hosted a significant computer array with multiple monitors.

Emily met Rylan's somber gaze. The sheriff waved her toward an open doorway at the side of the bullpen.

"We need to talk."

She followed him into a longish room with a large table taking up most of the space. He pulled out a chair for her and then took one next to hers.

"I'm sorry." He heaved a long breath. "We failed you and Oliver."

"Failed us? How can you think that when we're whole and healthy because of your preparations?"

Rylan shook his head. "The bug insured the bad guys knew our destination in advance."

"Granted, but you outmaneuvered them in the end, and that's what counts. So, thank you again. But I will say that the whole boxing-us-in scenario was a bit strange since they didn't start shooting."

"Not so strange if these people are as committed to keeping Oliver unharmed as we are. Without his presence, I'm not convinced they wouldn't have opened fire right away. As it is, I think they intended to hold us at gunpoint while they removed the baby and then shot us, but the arrival of our reinforcements scuttled the whole plan."

Emily's stomach somersaulted at an image of whole-sale slaughter inside a bullet-riddled pickup truck. Bile stung the back of her throat, and she swallowed against it.

"You could be right about that." Her voice had gone a bit hoarse. "So, basically, the baby saved our lives."

A grim smile stretched across Rylan's lips. "You could look at it that way. I think these guys want to get their hands on Oliver any way they need to go about it. Well, provided they can get away clean, which the arrival of more law enforcement did not allow. But now they'll have to move to Plan B. No, Plan C, actually, because the attempt at the hospital failed also. Right about now I'm sure they're getting extremely frustrated. Whoever is the mastermind behind this must be pulling out his hair."

"'A mastermind'?" An image of a sinister figure seated at a desk rubbing his hands together in a darkened office appeared in her mind's eye, but the mental picture was no memory, only a clichéd product of the imagination. "Of course, there's got to be someone pulling the strings behind the scenes. I don't think the muscle is coming up with these devious plans and resources on their own." A wry laugh spurted out between Emily's lips. "I hope Mr. Bossman is ripping himself bald." Now, *there* was a satisfying mental image. She leaned toward the sheriff. "So, what's next?"

"That's what we need to figure out. Keeping you here in the department headquarters indefinitely is neither practical for us nor comfortable for you."

"Why does our protection have to fall entirely on

Buck County? What about another agency like the US Marshals Service? Don't they protect people?"

"I've been in touch with them, and witness protection has guidelines your situation doesn't fulfill yet. The marshals are not *un*interested, but they're also not ready to step up until there's proof that you witnessed a murder."

"Like needing a body to turn up." The words tasted sour on her tongue.

He nodded, and she sighed.

"I certainly don't *want* someone to have been murdered, but the lack of a dead person leaves Oliver and me in a tough situation…and your county, as well. I just wish I could remember!" Emily's hands balled into fists.

Rylan's warm palm settled over one of them, and he offered a gentle squeeze. His large, sun-bronzed fingers completely encircled her pale, petite fist. A knot deep inside her unfurled as her hand relaxed in his. Something about the sheriff set her at ease at the same time her attraction meter went off the charts.

"When the time is right, you'll remember," he said.

His gentle words spread a balm over her frazzled nerves. She swallowed a lump in her throat.

"I hope so. I have this impression I used to be able to trust God with anything—especially the serious stuff. But something changed, and now…" Her voice trailed away as she stared at the table's woodgrain as if it might produce answers.

"'Used to'?"

Emily lifted her head and gazed into his intelligent eyes. Their steely hue was softened by—what? Compassionate interest? He was a good man, and she'd brought deadly problems to his doorstep. She dropped her gaze to the tabletop once more. How could she explain herself? She had to try.

"I have this overpowering sense that something awful happened to me *before* all this, with a dead body and fleeing with Oliver from men with guns. Whatever took place gutted everything I thought I knew about God, myself and others. I can't remember any specifics yet, but I know something happened like I know my own—" She caught herself short from finishing the sentence and spurted a laugh. "I'd better say like I know *your* name rather than my own because I can't remember even that most basic thing about myself."

The sheriff frowned and removed his hand from hers. Emily felt the loss of contact in her core.

"What if this deep trauma that occurred before the danger is the real reason your mind won't let you recall who you are and your past life?" he asked.

Emily sucked in a breath. The notion had flitted across her thoughts before. Was it truly possible her psyche was taking advantage of the concussion to protect itself? "Are you saying maybe I don't remember because subconsciously I can't bear to face the pain in my life?"

He nodded. "How do you feel about that idea?"

She pursed her lips then shook her head and let out a sigh. "If I could get online, I could research the issue. I'm good at that."

"What?"

"Research."

"How do you know?"

"I don't…" Her sentence trailed away. "I must have

training in this area, because I'm confident in my abilities."

Rylan clucked his tongue. "Maybe that's a clue as to your occupation, but part of your discharge instructions was cautious use of electronics for a while. I know because I had a concussion a while back, and I was told that, too."

Emily let out a frustrated growl. "At least we could ask Doc Laura if this idea has any psychiatric soundness. As an MD rather than a psychiatrist, she might not have the background to answer, but she might know whom to ask if my conscious desire to remember can be undermined by my subconscious desire to forget."

"That's a good way of putting it."

"But it's not the most crucial question."

"What is?"

"If I did witness a murder, I can understand why the perpetrators want me dead. But how does that make Oliver such a focus of interest?" She leaned toward the sheriff. "*Why* does some shadowy power-player want to take possession of my son? I believe if we knew the answer to that question, everything would become clear."

At her words, a jolt passed through Rylan. Not only was Emily correct in identifying the central question, but for the first time, she'd referred to Oliver as her son without an instant's hesitation. Did that mean her maternal instincts had resurfaced through her repressed memories? Or had looking after Oliver these past couple of days awakened the motherhood instinct that was already there? According to Doc Laura, the amount of healing Emily had done from the cesarean did not match Oliver's age. But if Ollie was not Emily's child, they were left with another big question: Where was the infant to whom she'd given birth? These were huge questions only slightly less vital to the current dangerous situation than the one Emily had posed.

"When will we get the results from the DNA test?"

Emily's words yanked Rylan out of his musings.

He offered her a lopsided smile. "Funny you should ask that. I was just thinking along those lines. We overnighted the swabs to the state forensic lab yesterday, but our urgency isn't likely to match theirs. With their backlog, we'll be doing well to get results in a matter of weeks rather than a matter of days, like some private labs can manage."

Emily caught her lower lip between her teeth and shook her head. "If only I had access to my money, I'd pay for the private test. Surely I have a bank account somewhere, but without access to that, I need to be gainfully employed. There will be hospital bills and childcare expenses." Her hands pressed against her temples as her breath came in little pants. "What am I going to do?"

Rylan folded his hands around her shoulders. "Look at me, Emily." She obeyed, and a measure of calm began to overtake the panic in her eyes. "You don't need to think about those things today. When the time comes to deal with the issues, the answers will be there. Right now, you need to concentrate on rest and recovery—and looking after Oliver, but you'll receive help with that also. This is a small town. Everyone knows about you and Ollie, and they're all on your side."

Emily's bottom lip began to quiver, and a tear made

its way down one cheek as she blinked rapidly. Rylan resisted the intimate impulse to gently wipe it away with his thumb. What was the matter with him? She was a victim under protection, not a girlfriend prospect, as much as a part of him had begun to wish their relationship didn't need to be confined to the professional. He needed to maintain hard focus. This was not a situation where he could relax.

"You're right," she said. "I do need to rest and be patient. I can't thank you and this community enough for your good care of Oliver and me."

Rylan withdrew his hands from her shoulders. "You should go lie down on the sofa in my office and catch a nap before the baby wakes up."

"All right." Her tone was meek, and she stood up. Dark shadows under her eyes proclaimed that she was still far from 100 percent. "Let me know if there are any further breaks in the case."

Emily left the room shoulder slumped and with a weary gait. Rylan followed on her heels until they reached the door to his office. She offered him a sober nod and went inside. He pulled the door closed and turned toward the department members working at their desks. Heads swiveled toward him as he walked past. When he reached the front of the room near the door to the dispatcher's station, he stopped and met their gazes.

"Any results on that search for a helicopter flying through the area?"

Head shakes and frowns met his inquiry.

"Okay. But keep trying to contact anyone and everyone from the ranches to see if they spotted a flyover. If so, we'll at least get an idea of what direction they were heading. Also, get the word out in the community to watch for strangers, especially groups of strangers. Drover's Creek is hardly a tourist destination, so there won't be that many unknowns running around town. I'd like us to get ahead of anything that's being planned, not keep playing catch-up."

Sarah nodded. "You got it, Sheriff. Whoever these yahoos are, they have no idea how strongly a small town can pull together when a threat rolls in."

Sounds of assent rippled through the room.

"And the small-town grapevine beats five-gig speed," Steve added.

Everyone chuckled, and even Rylan smiled despite the heaviness in his gut. Nothing in his career had prepared him for the conundrum of protecting a pair of strangers from a hidden threat coming after them for an unknown reason while also trying to determine if the hint of a murder witnessed was fact or fiction. Not to mention protecting his county from ruthless and resourceful attackers, who could well leave collateral damage in their attempts to achieve their objectives. If only he knew the real names of the people he was protecting or the mastermind behind the attacks or the person who may have been murdered. Then he might have an idea about the motive behind it all. Working this case was like swimming through the mud with one arm tied behind his back.

Rylan shook himself and turned on his heel. At Annie's station, he paused, and she looked up from her computer screen.

"Do you have a phone number for Centaur Financial Group?"

She gave it to him, and he punched the number into his cell phone. Taking a seat beside her, he waited for the call to go through. A pleasant-voiced woman answered and seemed quite startled when he informed her about the SUVs rented in their company name that had recently been in Drover's Creek, Wyoming. She passed his call up the chain, and a brusque woman who identified herself as the CFO denied any knowledge of the rentals and claimed none of the names given by the men in the vehicles matched Centaur's employees.

"You can be certain," she snapped, "that we will be pursuing this matter with the rental company and our own legal team. No one should be conducting potentially illegal activity in our name."

The call ended with her promise to inform him of developments that might help Buck County locate the impostors. Rylan wasn't going to hold his breath for that to happen. The situation was fraught with too much potential embarrassment for the corporation. He told Annie to keep digging into Centaur Financial Group and to have Steve check to see if the names given by the men in the Escalades were genuine or connected to identity theft or outright false IDs. Then he rose, stretching his back and shoulders.

"I'm going to meet Big Dave for lunch to share updates and strategize the next steps," he told the dispatcher. "Our guests are sleeping in my office, and I know everyone will keep a good eye on them."

"You can count on us," Annie answered.

"You have no idea how grateful I am."

The woman beamed at him. "Get outta here." She waved him away.

When he reached the front exit door, he paused and gazed out an adjacent window. The sun was busy shining, as it did most days here in the desert. The department-headquarters building sat back a block from the main highway, but many businesses lined the street in both directions. He was in sight of a feedstore, a grocery store, a veterinary clinic, a car dealership and the main law enforcement watering hole across the street, Barb's Café. The name was as no-nonsense as the food was home-cooked country goodness. Rylan recognized every vehicle parked along the street and knew each person in view going about their business, waving at one another or stopping to chat.

In fact, his good friend and neighbor, DeMarcus Dobbs, was sauntering into the feedstore. Dobbs was a fellow former Army Ranger, though his service dated a decade earlier than Rylan's. The man was the best long-distance rifleman he'd ever met. If things weren't so tense right now, Rylan would attempt to catch up with him to shoot the breeze.

But today wasn't like every other day. A malignancy grew somewhere dark and secret, ready to break out and deal death and destruction. Would he and his department be able to root it out before fatal damage happened to the citizens he was sworn to protect, especially the newest additions to the community—whoever they really were?

SIX

Heart full and warm, Emily gazed down at the baby boy happily sucking at his bottle as his pudgy little fingers wrapped around one of hers. Oliver stopped guzzling to coo up at her, and milk bubbles formed at the corners of his lips. Emily laughed. He answered with a grin and resumed drinking.

He was *her* child. No doubt about it. She didn't need the DNA-test results. How could love for him practically ooze from her pores if he wasn't hers?

"I'll protect you, my son," she murmured to precious Ollie. "No one will hurt you or snatch you on my watch."

Emily settled back against the cushions. A short time ago, Oliver's fussing to be fed had roused her from a nap on the sofa, which bore a faint scent of the sheriff's woodsy choice of soap. She had no idea how much time had passed, since there was no clock in the room or window through which to note the sun's height. Probably an hour or two, at most.

A soft rap sounded on the door panel, drawing her attention from the baby.

"Come in," Emily called out.

The door opened a foot or so, and Steve's head peered into the office.

"Good. I didn't wake you up. It's past the lunch hour, but I hadn't wanted to disturb your rest earlier. You must be hungry. What can I get you from the restaurant across the street?"

Emily smiled at the young man, and his round cheeks reddened. "Thank you. I'm starving. Would Barb's menu include a patty melt and fries? Ketchup on the side."

"Coming right up. I highly recommend Barb's apple pie, too."

"Sounds yummy. And an iced tea, please."

"Good choices." He grinned and withdrew, leaving the door slightly ajar.

Voices murmuring and keyboards clacking carried to Emily's ears while she burped Oliver; then the wiggling baby seemed to want to get down off her lap. She sat cross-legged on the floor beside his blanket. He practiced sitting up by himself while fingering, mouthing and shaking a baby toy of large plastic keys on a ring. Before leaving the hospital, Nurse Gwen had told her that people from the area had been coming by, continually donating items for Ollie's care, including a wide assortment of playthings. The kindness of the community that had welcomed her and Oliver seemed overwhelming, especially compared to the evil of others.

After a while, another knock came at the door, but instead of Steve, a short, plump older woman stepped inside upon Emily's permission. A curly, graying mop of reddish hair topped the woman's beaming face. In one hand, she held a white paper sack emanating savory odors, and the other hand clutched a large takeaway cup.

"I'm Annie, the daytime dispatcher," she said as Emily rose to her feet. "I've brought your lunch, dear."

"Thank you so much." Emily took the things from the woman's hands, but Annie's focus zeroed in on Oliver.

"He's adorable! May I hold him?"

"He loves attention and being held, and babies don't usually develop nervousness about strangers until eight or nine months, so give it a shot."

Emily maintained her smile at the older woman, but inwardly she questioned herself. How did she know that detail about infants? Somewhere in her unremembered life she must have studied infant development. Probably as a prospective mother. That would be normal. She relaxed as Annie scooped Oliver into her sturdy arms.

Emily took a seat at Rylan's massive desk. Judging from the scuffed-up condition of the aged wood, the sheriff probably wouldn't mind the chunky piece of furniture doubling as a table. Emily bit into her steaming sandwich, and flavor exploded on her tongue.

"This is fantastic!" she exclaimed around a mouthful.

Annie grinned as she took a seat on the sofa with the baby. "Barb's cookin' is the best in the county."

"I don't doubt you a bit."

While she ate, Emily scanned her environment. The minimalist room reflected its owner's no-nonsense, down-to-earth personality. The area was more cozy than roomy, with the sofa and a guest chair consuming most of the space not occupied by the big desk. A tall filing cabinet sat in the corner opposite the sofa. The desk supported a computer monitor, with a keyboard attached below the desktop and above the knee space. The inbox on the corner of the desk held a teetering stack of files, suggesting the sheriff might be putting off paperwork to deal with the extraordinary situation she and Oliver represented. Then again, maybe he always had that many files awaiting attention.

"You've livened up this little town considerably." Annie bounced a chortling Oliver on her knee.

"Not in a good way, I'm afraid." Emily's appetite ebbed.

"That bit's not your fault. It's amazin' to me how often victims feel to blame for the aggressor's bad actions. I'm no psychologist, but I figure a humble conscience is one more difference between the creeps who commit crimes while blamin' everyone else for their problems."

Emily blinked at the older woman. "I never thought about it that way. You may not have a psychology degree, but you're full of wisdom." She resumed enjoying her meal.

"Thank you, dear." The woman rose, set Oliver on his blanket and handed him a new toy. "I'd better get back to my duty station. Stevie's coverin', but he'd rather continue his research into those guys in the Escalades and rampin' up our missin' person's research. We've widened our inquiries—lookin' for a looker, so to speak."

"Someone missing me, you mean?"

Annie's gaze landed on her, steady and gentle. "You don't fit any kind of demographic of a person no one would miss, honey. There's got to be someone, whether they've reported you missin' yet or not. We'll keep those feelers out there until we get a nibble. Don't you worry 'bout that."

The older woman hustled out but left the door part-way open. Emily gathered the garbage from her meal and stuffed it into the paper sack in which it had arrived. Then she sat staring at the door. She didn't hear Rylan's voice; he must be out. A hollow sensation crept into her chest. Did it really matter to her whether he was near? Apparently it did. Her precarious mental and emotional state identified him with safety…and hope.

The man radiated competence and determination. If he couldn't figure out what was going on and put a stop to it, who would? The friendly dispatcher could well be wrong. Try as she might, Emily could dredge up no sense of anyone currently close to her in her life like a husband, siblings or parents. Surely she would know if she had a deep connection to someone else even though she couldn't remember precisely who. What, then, did that mean regarding Oliver's father? Was he no longer in their lives? Emily had no answers. As far as she knew, Sheriff Rylan and his team might be the only people who cared what happened to her and her son.

As if her thoughts had drawn him, his voice suddenly carried to her, greeting his staff. Heavy footfalls headed in the direction of the office. Then a knock came that pushed the door wider but not all the way open.

"We're here, Sheriff," she said. "Come on in. This is your office, after all."

His tall figure stepped inside, and he offered a smile. "Not as long as you and the baby need it."

Emily's stomach curdled. Was her life reduced to skulking in a borrowed office?

"Maybe you should put us up in a hotel room for now. At least until we figure out what's next. You've chased a group of ambushers out of your county. Surely there will be some respite before anything will be tried again."

Rylan studied her soberly. "You're a gutsy lady—you've shown that from the beginning. But I'm not ready to risk having you out in the public eye. We're putting together another safe house, and we'll transport you there after dark."

From the doorway came the sound of a clearing throat. The dispatcher's stocky figure walked into the office and closed the door behind her.

"She's got a safe house," Annie said. "My place. It's across the street behind this building. Not only can we sneak these two over there pretty easily, but even if someone managed to discover their location, they'd be loony tunes to mount an assault mere yards from law enforcement headquarters."

Silence blanketed the room as Emily gaped at the motherly dispatcher, and Rylan's gaze swept from Annie to Emily and back again.

"Are you sure about this, Annie? It's brilliant but…" His voice trailed off.

"Never been more certain."

"No!" Emily burst out. "I can't ask you to risk—"

"You're not askin', honey—I'm sayin'." For a woman who exuded gentleness from top to toe, Annie allowed no argument.

The sheriff's face split into a big grin, like that of a man with an unexpectedly lighter burden. Emily's heart turned over, and she quickly directed her gaze toward Oliver. Best she keep reminding herself this little guy was the only male she had time for in her life right now.

Rylan pulled aside the edge of the curtain over the picture window in his dispatcher's home and gazed out onto the quiet, darkened street. Streetlights at either end of the block spread a pale glow across the sidewalk in front of the modest craftsman-style house. No unaccounted-for vehicles sat parked on the street, and pedestrian traffic was nonexistent. Occasionally, a car or truck drove by, but most residents of Drover's Creek were winding down their day toward slumber in preparation for the work scheduled for tomorrow.

Across the street, the fenced-in parking lot at the side of law enforcement headquarters was well lit. Within the wide, squat building, glimmers of light peeked between blinds from areas where night staff worked. No one outside the station knew he'd posted a watcher in the darkened rear entryway with a window view of Annie's house. If nothing happened all night—the preferred outcome—the assignment would be tedious in the extreme and would keep an officer off normal patrol.

A sigh crept out between Rylan's lips. That kind of surveillance could continue only so long without creating undue strain on his staff and leaving the community less protected than it should be. They needed a more permanent solution to the problem of Emily and Oliver's safety, but time seemed to be on the bad guys' side. All they'd have to do is wait until his department inevitably let down their guard and then pounce. Or maybe even create some sort of catastrophic distraction elsewhere in town that would pull his people away from protecting the pair of lost strangers in their midst. A shudder ran through Rylan's frame.

"We'll be fine." Annie's voice came from near his shoulder.

Rylan let go of the curtain and turned toward the others in the living room. Oliver was absent because he was already asleep for the night in a portable crib in the guest bedroom. Emily gazed at Rylan from a perch on the edge of a country-floral armchair, her unease clear in her stiff posture. His dispatcher distracted him by extending a plate of homemade chocolate chip cookies toward him. Not about to wave the chewy goodness away, he helped himself to one. Annie sent him a nod and turned with the plate toward her houseguest.

"I shouldn't," Emily said, "but these look fantastic."

"Trust me," Rylan said through a bite. "They are."

Emily took a cookie, and Annie set the plate on the sturdy wooden coffee table in front of the sofa.

"You're welcome to seconds," she said. "I'm going to run a nice, hot bath for Mommy here."

"Thank you." Emily's face brightened. "I can hardly wait. You're pampering me too much."

Annie clucked her tongue. "No such thing, dear." The woman hustled from the room.

Rylan locked eyes with Emily. Silent seconds stretched between them, and then she dropped her gaze and slumped into the cushy seat.

"I know you can't guard me forever. I wish there was some way we could be proactive at catching these people. If we could get someone in custody, maybe they would tell us what's going on."

"I agree with everything you've said, but there is no *we* in dirtbag-catching. Leave that to my department."

Emily narrowed her eyes at him. "You have a plan in mind."

"Just the rudiments."

"Please tell me. It isn't like I don't have a right to know what's being done on Oliver's and my behalf."

Rylan quirked a half smile and took a seat on the sofa adjacent to Emily. "Technically, you don't have a *right* to know law enforcement's plans, but I'll grant you have a vested interest." He studied her earnest face. "Your suggestion about keeping you at a hotel has given me a glimmer of an idea of how to draw these lowlifes out."

"You mean like moving us there in plain sight and then catching whoever comes for us?"

"Not you and certainly not Oliver. I'm thinking more along the lines of planting a look-alike in a room with a baby doll in an infant seat."

Emily pursed her lips and stared pensively at a random spot in the corner. Rylan's heart panged at the delicate planes of her face. The woman was anything but fragile, but she embodied dainty grace—an incongruent contrast to his own rough-hewn exterior. Good thing their relationship was only professional. He wouldn't let his attraction to her affect his judgment. She'd never be interested in him, anyway.

"I like the idea." Her gaze returned to capture his. "But I can't allow someone to impersonate me."

"What do you mean?"

"Is there anyone in your department—city or county—whose build would mimic mine?"

"No, but—"

"Then you'd have to ask a civilian to play the part of me, and that's just as bad as letting me do it in the first place."

An objection hovered on the tip of Rylan's tongue, but he couldn't find the words to deny her observation, because there weren't any.

"It's settled, then." She jerked a nod. "Someone can look after Oliver here at Annie's house while I quite publicly check into a hotel with a baby carrier in tow. When do you want to start dangling me as bait?"

"Not tonight." His words came out gruff.

The idea was excellent; the means they would have to use stank. Every molecule of himself hated deliberately placing this woman in the path of violent people. She was at risk enough without purposely enhancing the danger.

"Agreed," she said. "Not tonight. I'm exhausted right now and need a good night's sleep. But how about I check into a hotel of your choice tomorrow afternoon?"

Rylan sighed and dipped his head in defeat. "There aren't many places for travelers to stay in Drover's Creek. We're a bit off the beaten path. One of those chain hotels is located in an area near a couple of restaurants and a big-box store. I don't like that option because there's a lot of civilian activity nearby. Or there's a bed-and-breakfast in a residential area."

"And that's a bad idea, too, because of all the neighbors."

"Right, but there's a little mom-and-pop motel on the

edge of town that might work out. Out beyond the building with the connected rooms, they have several stand-alone cabins. I don't know if the owners will agree to let us use one of their units for a stakeout, but I'll ask first thing tomorrow."

Emily let out a long breath. "We've got the start of a plan, then. I won't say I'm not a little frightened, but I'm more frightened to go on the way we are. I'm really angry, too." Her hands fisted. "What right do these people have targeting me and a helpless infant?"

"I'm angry, too, but one thing I've learned—crooks aren't worried about anyone else's rights."

Emily's lower lip quivered; then she stiffened it and reached out to touch his wrist where it lay on the sofa's armrest. A head-lightening buzz of electricity flowed through Rylan, but he refused to acknowledge the reaction.

"I can't say it enough, but thank you." She was soft and warm.

"My pleasure—*our* pleasure." Hopefully, she didn't notice his voice had gone husky. "On behalf of my department and me, we heartily wish none of this were happening to you and Oliver, but we're here for you."

"This whole community has proven that many times over. Buck County is full of the salt of the earth."

Rylan grinned. "We like to think so."

Their gazes locked, and Emily smiled back at him. He prayed the melting of his heart didn't show on the outside. Approaching footfalls broke her attention from him, and Rylan swallowed against a suddenly dry throat. What was with this teenage angsty attraction? He needed to get a grip. He'd been a widower for over five years, but he hadn't experienced significant interest in another woman until now. And it had to be *this* woman, who was about as off-limits as possible.

"Your bath awaits, darlin'," Annie announced.

Emily rose. "I'll see you tomorrow, Rylan. I hope you'll have good news for me about putting our plan into effect."

Annie shot him a hard look, though she said nothing as she turned and led Emily away up the hall.

Rylan got up and began double-checking the locks on all the doors and windows. Annie had no electronic security system installed, but not many in Buck County did. He'd make sure that surreptitiously changed tomorrow… along with all the other tasks on his list. The threat was unlikely to materialize tonight because it wasn't reasonable to suppose the bad guys knew their objectives' location.

Nevertheless, he'd be sleeping on Annie's generous sofa. His feet would dangle over the end, but that was a small price to pay for the opportunity to stand between Emily and Oliver and their nameless, faceless enemies. He'd already arranged for his neighboring rancher, DeMarcus, to come over and feed his horses and dog until further notice. Tomorrow night—provided he'd made all the arrangements by then—would be more harrowing. If any malicious watchers were in town, they'd know right where to find the woman they intended to kill. By God's grace, Rylan and his department would stand in their way and take them down.

SEVEN

Under the heat of the late-afternoon sun, Emily's skin prickled as she made her way toward the last of the motel's adjoining cabins in a row on the outskirts of Drover's Creek. One sweaty hand drew a suitcase wheelie while the other hand pushed the stroller with Oliver's infant seat snapped into it. A life-size and very realistic doll lay beneath the seat's straps.

Her footfalls tapped loudly in her ears, and her breathing came in harsh rasps. The wheels on the stroller and her case made *snick-snick* sounds as they rolled over cracks in the sidewalk. The smells of tarmac under the baking sun and a trace of pungent earthiness filled her nostrils. The sheriff had explained the earthy scent was from the feed mill a few blocks away.

With every nerve ending in Emily's body screaming at her to run and hide, it took all her willpower to maintain a normal pace. Even so, muscle tension turned her stride jerky and awkward. But if evil eyes were watching, perhaps they would expect to see signs of high-strung nerves in their quarry.

"You're doing great." Rylan's firm, deep voice in her earpiece steadied her.

Where exactly he was hiding, she didn't know, but she'd been assured he and a mix of three deputies and officers were nearby.

Emily didn't answer the sheriff's encouraging words. If someone hostile were watching, it wouldn't do for her to show she was talking to someone.

At last, she reached the front door of her cabin and fumbled to thread the old-fashioned metal key into the lock. *Get a grip.* She ordered her hand to stop shaking. The key turned, and the lock gave way with a soft click. Emily pushed the stroller over the threshold and then stepped into the twilight of a twelve-by-twelve room dimly illuminated by sunlight peeping in through partially closed window blinds. A mild odor of cleaning solution and floral air freshener hung in the air, assurance of the owner's care for cleanliness and pleasant ambience for their guests.

The space was tidy, and the queen-size bed was neatly made. The room also held a desk with a lamp on top, a dresser supporting a small TV and a miniature coffee maker, and a closet with the doors hanging open to reveal a few bare hangers.

Home, sweet home. Or maybe she should dub it *trap, sweet trap* and she was *bait, sweet bait.*

With a low groan, Emily rolled the stroller into a bare spot against the wall by the desk and then guided the small suitcase to a halt near the closet. The case didn't contain much—just a few changes of clothes rounded up by the ever-resourceful Annie and the toiletries supplied by the hospital. If only she could go shopping and pick out a few things for herself… But not only was she financially destitute, traipsing all over town wasn't in the plan. She wasn't supposed to hide, exactly, but her movements were proscribed to taking "the baby" out for a walk up and down the block. The activity was designed to serve additional notice to any watchers as to her location while keeping her away from most other civilians and providing a limited area to be surveilled by law enforcement.

Hopefully, the baited stakeout would require only one night, though there was no guarantee someone would come after her that quickly or even at all. Maybe yesterday's failure had convinced them to give up. *Sure, and I'm the queen of England.* Whoever wanted to kill her and grab Oliver had shown no signs of being the sort to give up. Thus far, their approaches had been audacious and resourceful. Emily and her protection detail could expect nothing less if hostiles came for her at the motel. *Please, God, help us to be prepared.*

"Situation report." The sheriff's firm-voiced request sounded in her ear, carrying a hint of tension. Probably over the length of time it had taken for Emily to declare her well-being after entering the cabin.

"Sorry." Emily sighed. "Just taking a few minutes to orient myself. Situation report? Sitrep, for short. That's military terminology. Did you serve?"

Silence came back at her for several heartbeats. "Regular army grunt for four years," he said. "Then a Ranger for another four. You recognize the lingo. Did *you* serve?"

"No...at least, I don't think so. But someone I loved..."

Emily's voice trailed away as her pulse rate went into overdrive, and her rib cage squeezed in on her heart. Was she remembering something? She reached out mentally to grab the impression and make it something solid, but the notion slipped away like oil through her fingers.

"Someone close to you was in the military? Who?" Rylan's tone had gone urgent.

"I don't know!" The words were spat from her lips in a snarl. "I can't think. I don't want—"

"Take it easy. It's okay. You'll remember when the time is right."

Emily fought to control her breathing and calm herself, but her head began to pound, and dizziness swept through her. The effects of her concussion were not gone. The doc had said it could be weeks before she was 100 percent.

"I think I need to rest for a bit." She slumped into a sitting position on the edge of the bed.

"No problem. Remember, there are sensors around the small window in the bathroom to alert us in the unlikely event that an extremely slender assailant might try to access the cabin from that direction. And there's a pressure plate under the mat outside the front door that will emit a silent alarm and notify us of an approaching intruder. There are no other access points, and we've got eyes on the structure from every direction."

"Thank you." She slipped off her shoes. "I know everyone is doing the best they can to keep me safe. What about Oliver and Annie? Have you checked in with them lately?"

A deep, mellow chuckle answered her. The sound soothed as much as it attracted her. Everything about the sheriff was growing on her, which was a dismaying issue for a woman who didn't know her own identity or life situation. But she couldn't blame him for her foolish feelings; he'd been nothing but professional with her. Nor could she fault his amusement with her question. It had scarcely been a half hour since she'd kissed Oliver goodbye.

"Oliver and Annie are enjoying an early supper together. They're fine. Are you hungry? You could order out, and I'll make sure the delivery person is trustworthy."

"Maybe later. I feel drained right now. I'm going to lie down and close my eyes for a few minutes."

"Understandable. You're still recovering from a serious concussion. Don't push yourself. Remember, we're on overwatch out here."

"Thanks again," Emily murmured and allowed herself to stretch out on a surprisingly comfortable mattress with a pillow that half swallowed her head.

Of course, she wasn't going to sleep. It was too early, and the situation was too tense. How would she even allow herself to sleep when it was the right time for bed? No, she would just rest her eyes for a bit and let her frazzled emotions settle.

She breathed in. She breathed out. In. Out. Her pulse whooshed softly in her ears. Gradually, the pain in her head faded. She should get up now. She should…

Someone knocked on the door. A distant sound because she was in bed, drowsing. The knocking grew in volume. Insistent.

She forced her eyelids open. The bedroom appeared around her, sepia-toned but familiar. The knocking became pounding, and she heaved her bulk off the bed. She shouldn't be getting up. Her ob-gyn had put her on best rest. But there was no one else in the house to answer the door.

Dressed in her comfy sweatpants and a loose shirt, she shuffled out of the darkened bedroom into the hallway and blinked at the unaccustomed light. It was still the afternoon. So much enforced relaxation made it difficult to keep track of time.

"I'm coming!"

Her voice seemed a futile croak against the hammering on the door, and she moved as if attempting to make way through a viscous fluid congealing around her and holding her fast. At last, she arrived at the door and reached her hand toward the knob.

Don't do it. Don't let them in. *The words rang like an urgent litany in her head.*

But as if she had no control over her own body, her hand turned the knob and then flung the door wide.

A male and a female in dress uniforms, their caps under their arms, stood straight and tall, gazing at her with solemn eyes. At that moment, she knew, and her world imploded. Agony ripped through her belly. Arms reached for her as primal screams rent her throat.

Emily jerked upright in bed, her own screams echoing in her ears. Her forehead slammed into something firm that yielded with a snap and a high-pitched angry curse. The same hammering on the door and dim light as in her dream filled the cabin. But the arms reaching for her were anything but friendly and concerned.

Angry eyes blazed at her as iron fingers closed around her throat, choking her cries. Something sharp jabbed toward her.

Once more, Rylan slammed his shoulder into the motel cabin door, and this time it flew open to crash against the side wall. He charged through and rammed into the slender figure standing over Emily with a weapon lifted. The flying tackle sent him to the floor with the assailant beneath him.

The breath gushed from the attacker in a long squeak, but she—yes, definitely a female—managed to jam her weapon into his shoulder. Ignoring the sharp jab, Rylan swept the assailant's arms away from him, flipped her over onto her stomach and gathered her wrists together behind her back. As he applied the cuffs, he began officially informing her of her arrest.

"Stop!"

Emily's urgent cry froze him in place and halted his words. With her hands lifted, palms outward, she stood over him and his prone suspect.

"Don't make another move," she told him in a harsh whisper.

Then she reached out and plucked the sharp object from the flesh over his shoulder joint.

"Thank You, Lord," she wheezed out on a long exhale of breath. "She didn't get a chance to depress the plunger."

Rylan squinted up at the object Emily held gingerly between two fingers. It was a syringe with some sort of clear liquid inside. His throat muscles tightened. Sure, he'd stopped the murder attempt against Emily, but she'd returned the favor by saving *his* life.

Rylan's narrow focus on apprehending the would-be assassin widened to take in the commotion going on outside the cabin door—shouts, engines revving and squealing tires, set to the beat of whirling red and blue lights. He hauled his cuffed suspect to her feet, dragged her squirming, cursing figure to the open doorway and peered out in time to see a panel van escape the motel parking lot by ramming through a hedge, off-road, and clipping the bumper of a squad car blocking access to the street. Crumpling metal moaned and glass shattered with the collision. Then the van surged onto the highway out of town. A sheriff's SUV and the squad car with the crumpled bumper sped after it, sirens wailing.

"The baby's car seat is gone," Emily said, her tone thin and high, as if short of air.

Rylan could hardly blame her for struggling to breathe normally right after the violence she'd experienced. Glancing over toward the stroller, he confirmed Emily's declaration. The frame sat empty of the infant seat.

He smirked at the dark-haired female in his custody. She responded with an inky-eyed glare.

"I hope your accomplice likes playing with dolls," he said.

The woman's jaw slackened; then her lips clamped shut in a thin line as if daring him to get a word out of her. Twin lines of drying blood marked the spaces between her nostrils and her lips, and her nose appeared to be swelling. Rylan frowned. No way had his actions caused that injury.

He turned his gaze toward Emily. "Did you get a punch in?"

Her fingers went to her forehead. "No, I sat up suddenly and accidentally headbutted her."

Rylan grinned. "Good for you."

She cupped her forehead in her hands. "Didn't do my concussion any favor."

Another law enforcement vehicle rolled into the

parking lot and stopped outside Emily's cabin. Deputy Lawrence stepped out and came toward them, one hand resting on the gun fastened to her belt. With everything that was going on, he'd allowed her to come off desk duty a little early.

"Everything okay here?" Sarah asked.

"We're good." He stepped out the door of the motel cabin, his prisoner in tow. "Take this suspect to the lockup and book her." He thrust the attempted murderer toward the rear of the county sheriff's unit.

"My pleasure." Sarah jerked a nod and opened the back door to receive the guest of the county into the caged area.

"Read the suspect her rights as you go," Rylan said.

"No problem." Sarah shut the door on their captured crook and set her gaze on something behind him. "Emily, how are you doing?"

The woman stepped up beside Rylan, the top of her head barely reaching above his shoulder.

"I'm fine. *Now* I am, anyway." Emily rubbed the bandage over her head wound and then peered up at him. "I can't believe I laid down and went to sleep. I'm so sorry."

"You have nothing to be sorry for. As usual, you acted with courage and resourcefulness. This is the second time you've saved my life. Thank you for your quick thinking."

"Likewise." She dipped her head in a gracious nod.

He grinned at her, and she smiled back, nearly shattering his willpower. His arms physically ached to wrap her in them. To offer comfort, of course—and maybe some further reason he wasn't willing to acknowledge. Rylan tore his attention from her as the county evidence-collection van glided into the parking lot.

"I'll leave you to it," Sarah said then climbed into her cruiser and rolled out.

Steven emerged from the crime scene van with an ancillary staffer named Ted. Rylan told them about the syringe with its ominous contents. Emily said she'd left the item on the TV stand, and the pair went inside, snapping on nitrile gloves and pulling out evidence bags.

"Take me to Oliver." Emily's gaze beseeched Rylan.

"You got it." He turned and poked his head into the cabin. "Hand me Emily's wheelie, would you, Steven? There's nothing evidentiary about it."

The younger man complied, and Rylan took the case. "This way." He motioned Emily toward the gas station next to the motel/cabin complex. "My unmarked sedan is parked in the shadows over there. I didn't dare drive my pickup, because those goons who accosted us the other day had seen it and would no doubt have passed the description up the chain."

"Wherever that chain leads," Emily said as they walked to the vehicle with the westering sun warming their backs.

She fell silent, but her stiff posture and jerky steps betrayed an understandable tension. Soon they were cruising through town on a course toward the law enforcement headquarters, and her shoulders seemed to relax.

"I'm going to take you back to the cop shop for now." He glanced toward her. "Then, after darkness falls, we'll smuggle you across the street to Annie's house like we did yesterday."

She whipped her head toward him. "You seriously think more watchers are lurking out there?"

Rylan frowned. "We're up against a greater degree of ruthless resourcefulness than I've ever experienced, and I don't want to take unnecessary risks."

"Like dropping me off directly at Annie's house."

"Exactly."

"Okay, I can see that, but I hate being away from Ollie one more second than necessary." She spoke the words as if they tasted bitter.

"I totally get that. We'll make things as expeditious as possible."

"At least I'll be right there in the office when you interview my attacker. I'd love to be a part of that."

Rylan pursed his lips, mulling her implied request. "That request is outside normal protocol, but in this circumstance, I'll allow you to be behind the one-way glass in company with an officer or deputy. Maybe the conversation will jog a memory."

"Thank you." Her small fists bunched in her lap, and then the fingers loosened as she inhaled a deep breath and let it out in a slow whoosh. "How did my attacker get into the cabin? Did she go through the back window? She was thin enough to make it through the dinky bathroom window."

Rylan shook his head. "If I hadn't seen the full-frontal assault myself, I wouldn't believe it. Barely a half hour after you went into the cabin, the suspects' van whipped into the lot, skidded to a halt outside your door and two people leaped out. I was already on my way at a run, but the female jabbed something into the door lock that let them in almost instantly. The guy darted inside and rushed back out with the baby seat. He spotted me coming, turned the door lock on the unit, slammed it shut and then practically dived into the van. Things were happening in hyperdrive all at once, with patrol cars closing in. I broke into your room, and you know the story from there."

Rylan darted a sideways glance at his passenger. Her head was bowed, her face pale, yet her jaw jutted resolutely. He couldn't describe Emily as fearless; she was terrified and rightfully so. But persistence in doing right in the face of fear was the highest manifestation of courage.

She'd volunteered to be bait, and they'd caught at least one bottom-feeder—maybe more if the pursuit of the van had resulted in arrests. Time would tell if they'd landed big fish or minnows. He suspected the latter, but at least his department had a hook into the situation that they'd utterly lacked before.

Please, God, let this progress lead us to answers that will keep Emily and Oliver safe.

EIGHT

Emily walked a step in front of a hovering Sheriff Rylan into the all-but-deserted headquarters building. No one hung out in the bullpen, but a feminine voice carried from the dispatcher's station. The sheriff headed in that direction, and Emily trailed him.

"Update on the fleeing van?" Rylan asked a slender twentysomething woman seated behind the bulletproof glass.

Emily hadn't met this person before, and the attractive female fixed her with a bright blue narrow-eyed gaze. Then the woman turned her attention toward Rylan, and her whole countenance softened as she brushed a strand of long, lush brown hair back over her shoulder. The subtly flirtatious move spoke volumes about the woman's intentions toward Rylan, though he had to be at least a decade older than her. The sheriff's businesslike demeanor didn't register a response in kind, and Emily suppressed a smile. Then she scolded herself. Why should it matter to her if another woman had designs on this man, whom she'd only known for a few days? Still, the shortness of the time since they'd met seemed not to matter to her heart that quickened whenever he stepped into her presence.

"The pursuit team just called it in," the dispatcher said, deadpan, and then grinned. "We got him. The driver tried to take a turn at high speed on two wheels and flipped the vehicle into a steep ditch. He's in custody but stone-cold out of it with what may be serious injuries. An ambulance is on the way." The woman grimaced. "Goes to show people should always wear their seat belts."

"Thanks for filling in, Mandy." The sheriff gave her a nod. "You do a great job. Please keep me informed."

"Will do."

By the smirk on the woman's face, Emily judged that if Mandy had been a cat, she would have been purring.

"Oh, by the way—" Rylan turned toward Emily "—I haven't introduced the two of you to each other. Emily, this is Amanda King, our night dispatcher. Amanda, this is Emily, our—"

"Wandering stranger taken in by a bighearted town," Emily finished for him.

Rylan chuckled, his gaze warm on her. "I was going to say protectee, but your description works for now."

Emily darted a glance at the dispatcher, whose face had flushed a rosy hue around eyes like chips of blue ice. Now, if Mandy were a cat, Emily judged the woman would have her claws unsheathed. A tremor went through her. The Bible described jealousy as "cruel as the grave." Did she need to watch her back here?

She schooled her expression to neutrality and extended her hand toward Mandy. "Pleased to meet you.

I can't say enough about how well this town has treated Oliver and me."

At this reminder that Emily was a mother and possibly even had a husband somewhere out there, the dispatcher's countenance softened. Mandy briefly clasped Emily's hand but ended the contact almost as quickly as it had begun. Emily had the sense that she was now on probation with the young woman.

"Come with me." Rylan motioned toward Emily and set off back through the squad room.

She followed him to his office, where he took a seat behind his desk and booted up his computer. Emily settled onto his familiar sofa. She was safe here like no other place since she'd awakened in the hospital. The only thing lacking was her arms around Oliver.

"I'm going to check on Sarah's progress booking the suspect into the system." He began clicking through entries on his screen, then let out a grunt. "No identification on her person, and she refused to give a name or any other personal details. However-r-r... Hah!" Rylan smacked his palms against his desk, and Emily stiffened. "Sarah immediately entered the suspect's fingerprints into IAFIS—the Integrated Automated Fingerprint Identification System—and Ms. Needle has a record. So much for keeping her mouth shut. Her whole background is on file." Rylan tapped a button on his keyboard, and a printer whirred to life out in the bullpen.

He got up and headed in that direction without a glance toward her.

Emily rose and stayed on his heels. "Who is she?"

Rylan snatched several sheets of paper from the

printer and scanned through them. Emily folded her arms, tamping down irritation with the sheriff in his cop zone, tuning her out. She cleared her throat. He lifted his head and blinked at her like he'd forgotten her presence.

A smile quirked one side of his lips. "Her name is Leota Grimes, a thirty-six-year-old with dual Canadian and US citizenship. Up until six years ago, she was a nurse in Calgary, Alberta."

"A nurse? How horrible that someone who'd pledged to save lives would turn to attempted murder with a tool of the trade, a syringe."

Rylan shook his head. "Not the first time such a thing has happened."

"How did this woman go from nursing to being complicit with killing?"

"She disappeared from Canada after she was suspected of stealing drugs from her hospital's pharmacy. Then, three years ago, she was arrested in Denver as part of a drug trafficking ring. That's the first time her prints appeared in the United States system, either criminal or health-care related. We don't have direct access to Canadian health-care worker background checks that include fingerprints on file." He flipped a page in his printout. "Leota just got out of prison a couple of months ago. Looks like she'll be going back behind bars for a much longer stint this time."

Rylan's flurry of information entered Emily's ears and passed through her brain, but her mind had returned to one detail and gotten stuck on it.

"Canada. There's something…" Her voice drifted away, and she shook her head.

The sheriff's gaze narrowed on her. "You think you might be from Canada?"

"I don't know."

How Emily was coming to hate those three words, but there was nothing else to say. The black abyss in her psyche that held her memories stared back at her and gave up nothing.

"With your permission, I could send a request across the border and see if anything pops as far as your identity. I'm not sure how quickly they'll respond, but it might be worth a shot."

She jerked a nod. "Do it. In the meantime, what about this Leota Grimes? What can she tell us about who's after Oliver and me?"

"Let's go find out."

Stomach roiling, Emily followed the sheriff through a door into an annex to the main building. This first part of the annex was a rectangular room containing a station that looked like it was for booking, with a camera and backdrop for suspect photographing and a few gadgets on a counter, one of which was likely for electronic fingerprinting. At the far side of the room stood a barred portal that no doubt led to cells.

The change in atmosphere struck Emily like a physical blow. The squad room had been warm and welcoming, albeit businesslike, but this area held a chill and smelled of disinfectant, like a hospital but with a metallic overlay.

Deputy Lawrence turned from a computer desk in the corner of the room. "Did you get all the goodies?" she asked the sheriff.

He waved the sheaf of papers. "Excellent work, Sarah."

The woman nodded as he handed her the papers, and she got busy putting them and other items into a file folder.

"Where is our guest?" Rylan jerked his chin toward the custody area. "In a cell?"

"Waiting for you in the interview room." Sarah tilted her head toward another door next to a large window.

Emily drifted in that direction, stopped in front of the window and peered inside the room beyond. The woman now known as Leota, ex-nurse and drug dealer, sat at a metal table with her wrists cuffed to the tabletop. The woman's face was angled downward as she stared at her hands and picked at her cuticles.

A hard life had ravaged Leota's appearance. Rylan had said the woman was thirty-six years old, but she looked at least a decade older. However, the deep shadows under her eyes were more than signs of premature aging. Bruising had begun to form on either side of the woman's swollen nose. Emily hadn't meant to injure her assailant but couldn't bring herself to regret the accidental blow. The happy circumstance of jerking awake from a nightmare and colliding with Leota's face might have saved her from a fatal poke with a needle—assuming, of course, that the substance in the syringe was a deadly poison. But since someone clearly wanted her dead, it was a reasonable conclusion.

As if Leota sensed someone gazing at her from the other side of the one-way glass, she lifted her head and glared at the window. The woman's lips curled into a tooth-baring snarl beneath feral eyes.

Emily gasped and backpedaled into a solid object.

Whoof! Rylan. The man's large, warm hands closed around her shoulders. Standing with the top of her head tucked under his chin felt like—what? Home?

"You don't have to watch the interview," he said gently.

"Yes, I most certainly do." She pulled away and turned around to face him. "There are two things I desperately need. Number one, for Oliver and me to be safe, and number two, for me to recover my memories and my life. If hearing what this woman has to say might guide me toward either goal, I'm all ears, regardless of how difficult or painful new knowledge might be."

Rylan smiled down at her. Was she mistaken, or did his gaze hold both pride and tenderness? Before she could decide, the man seemed to give himself a shake. Then he headed toward the door to the interview room. Sarah intercepted him with the completed file. The sheriff accepted it and took the folder with him into the interview room.

Every muscle in Emily's body tensed. Were they finally about to get some answers? And if so, would these answers have anything to do with the dream she'd had right before the attack? She couldn't prove it, but the things she experienced in the dream were not nightmare whisps of imagination. She'd experienced every aspect of that dream in real life. However, the mere thought of talking about it, much less bringing forth the full memory, left her mouth dry and her limbs trembling.

Emily bit her lower lip against calling Rylen back and stiffened her knees against fleeing the scene. Maybe she *wasn't* strong enough to face whatever truth might come out.

* * *

Rylan closed the interview-room door and then halted, silently observing the suspect. She sat on the edge of her seat at the table, which stood perpendicular to the viewing window. At his appearance, the woman went rigid but maintained a stoic stare at the tabletop where her cuffed hands rested.

"Leota Grimes," he said, and a minuscule shudder passed through the woman's frame. "You're a long way from Denver and even farther away from Alberta, Canada. What brings you to Drover's Creek, Wyoming?"

"I don't have to tell you anything." The woman's words emerged in a smoker's growl, but she kept her eyes averted.

Rylan suppressed a smile. Denial was expected, but it hadn't come with the demand for a lawyer. If those words passed the woman's lips, the interview would be over. Everything within him rebelled at that thought. It was past time to glean some intel his department could sink its teeth into and find solutions.

He stepped forward and drew back the empty chair across from the suspect. The chair's legs grated against the cement floor. A tiny cringe in the woman's narrow shoulders didn't escape Rylan's observation. The suspect was teetering on a razor's edge of losing self-control. Aside from knowing she was in a world of legal trouble, she could well be entering withdrawals from her drug of choice. That status could work for or against the interview results.

For the recording Sarah would be starting from the outer room, he stated the date, time and circumstances of the interview. Then he recited the Miranda warning again for the record and asked if Leota understood. She mumbled assent as he took his seat and slapped the case folder onto the table. The woman's hands balled into fists, and she let out a high-pitched whimper.

"You're afraid," Rylan said. "You should be scared with an attempted murder charge pending, not to mention parole violation and resisting arrest. But you can help yourself by telling me everything you know about the attack today."

"I can't say." A muscle twitched in the woman's jaw, and her dark gaze darted in his direction and then down toward her hands again.

"Can't? Or won't? Your cooperation will look good in front of a judge."

"I don't know anything!" Leota sat up straight and glared at him. "I do what I'm told or else."

"Or else what?"

The woman shook her head like a dog shedding water and turned her gaze downward again. "You wouldn't understand."

"Try me."

Leota lifted her head slowly. "He threatened to cut me off if I didn't do what he said. I couldn't have that. I wouldn't survive."

Rylan regarded her steadily, not softening his expression but pondering her words. What a horror of an existence, to be so enslaved to a mind-altering substance that survival depended on obtaining it—or so it seemed to the addict.

"Who threatened to cut you off?"

"Double D, the van driver. Dennis Dorfman."

"He's your pusher?"

The woman nodded.

"Did you know he's in the hospital?"

Leota shook her head. "I guess he won't be fixing me up anymore." Every syllable dripped despair.

"We can provide methadone or something else appropriate to minimize the withdrawal discomfort, but you've got to give us some help here before we can get to that point."

Her gaze darted toward him and then away, her expression brightening the slightest bit. "I don't know much. Just that Double D said some big shot way up the supply chain needed urgent stuff done."

"Kidnapping a baby and killing a woman?"

Leota's jaw firmed. "I'm not admitting to anything."

"You won't have to. We've got you cold. Who is this drug kingpin?"

"Double D didn't say a name, but he was terrified of disappointing him. Like dripping-sweat scared." Her eyes began twitching from his face to the one-way glass and back again in a repetitive cycle. "This guy, he's ruthless. He'll kill you all to get what he wants."

"Why does he want the baby?"

The question hung in pregnant silence between them. It was unlikely the woman knew the answer to this pivotal issue, but he had to ask.

The muscles in Leota's throat flexed. "Double D said the whole thing was a matter of blood, whatever that means."

"As in, bloodline? Is this bigwig related to the infant?"

Something like an electrical charge passed through Rylan. Could it be that Emily was related to whoever wanted to kill her and take her baby? If so, recovering her memories might be crucial to her survival and Oliver's safety.

But Leota's face remained blank, and she rippled her shoulders in a shrug.

Soft rapping sounded on the one-way glass, and Rylan glanced in that direction. Either Sarah or Emily had something she urgently needed to impart to him. Gripping the file folder, Rylan headed for the door.

"I'll be right back." He was starting to think he'd gotten as much as he could from the sorry woman. She was clearly caught up in something much bigger than herself that she knew little about.

Rylan stepped out the door, and Emily moved close, her face pale and drawn.

"I don't believe it. The picture she's painting is just… off somehow. I'm quite sure I don't know any drug traffickers, much less someone high up in the pipeline, and if Oliver is mine, we're not related to this… this monster."

Rylan restrained himself from pointing out that they still didn't know for sure that Oliver was Emily's son. Instead, he touched her arm and offered an understanding smile.

"Even if either of you *were* related to this man, there's no guilt by association here. No taint to be worried about."

"I know that. I do, but—" She huffed and squared her shoulders. "Ask her about the murder I'm ninety percent sure I witnessed. Somehow that event is the key to why Oliver and I are here and in our current predicament."

Rylan nodded. "Good idea."

Sarah, standing a few paces behind Emily, mimicked his nod. "Fine instincts, there. Maybe we should deputize her."

At the compliment, Emily looked over her shoulder and smiled at the woman. "Thanks, but no thanks." A bit of color returned to her complexion. She gazed up at Rylan. "And thank you for believing in me."

"Always." He meant the pledge and yet still demanded objectivity of himself.

The integrity and courage Emily had consistently exhibited in this extremely tough situation argued convincingly for an innately trustworthy character, regardless of her memory's condition. For that reason, he would continue to give her the benefit of the doubt, despite a cop of any stripe's tendency toward suspicion.

With an inclination of his head toward Emily and Sarah, he headed back into the interview room. The suspect was now sitting slumped and loose-limbed in her chair, as if fear and dread had drained her of strength.

Rylan resumed his seat. "What do you know about a murder that took place in Burling, Wyoming, over a week ago?"

Leota's body went rigid. She lifted her hands, palms out, as high as the cuffs would allow. "Oh, no, no, no. You're not pinning that on me."

Rylan schooled his expression not to show the sudden heat coursing through him. Did a bloodhound who'd caught the scent feel like this?

"I didn't say we think you did it," he told her. "I want to hear what you know about it."

"Nothing. I wasn't there. I didn't have anything to do with it. Just heard stuff. Double D said—" The sus-

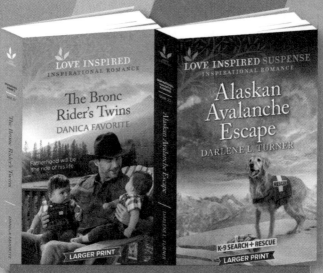

Get Free Books In Just 3 Easy Steps

Are you an avid reader searching for more books?
The **Harlequin Reader Service** might be for you! We'd love to send you up to **4 free books** just for trying it out. Just write **"YES"** on the **Free Books Voucher Card** and we'll send your free books and a gift, altogether worth over $20.

Step 1: Choose your Books

Try *Love Inspired® Romance Larger-Print* and get 2 books and fall in love with inspirational romances that take you on an uplifting journey of faith, forgiveness and hope.

Try *Love Inspired® Suspense Larger-Print* and get 2 books where courage and optimism unite in stories of faith and love in the face of danger.

Or *TRY BOTH*!

Step 2: Return your completed Free Books Voucher Card

Step 3: Receive your books and continue reading!

Your free books are **completely free**, even the shipping! If you continue with your subscription, you can look forward to curated monthly shipments of brand-new books from your selected series, always at a discount off the cover price! Plus you can cancel any time.

Don't miss out, reply today! Over $20 FREE value.

Free Books
Voucher Card

YES! I love reading, please send me more books from the series I'd like to explore and a free gift from each series I select.

More books are just 3 steps away!

Just write in "**YES**" on the dotted line below then select your series and return this Books Voucher today and we'll send your free books & a gift asap!

▶▶ *YES* ◀◀

Choose your books:

☐ **Love Inspired® Romance Larger-Print**
122/322 CTI G29D

☐ **Love Inspired® Suspense Larger-Print**
107/307 CTI G29D

☐ **BOTH**
122/322 & 107/307
CTI G29F

FIRST NAME

LAST NAME

ADDRESS

APT.#

CITY

STATE/PROV.

ZIP/POSTAL CODE

EMAIL ☐ Please check this box if you would like to receive newsletters and promotional emails from Harlequin Enterprises ULC and its affiliates. You can unsubscribe anytime.

LI/LIS-1123-OM_123ST

♦HARLEQUIN® Reader Service —**Here's how it works:**

▲ If offer card is missing write to: Harlequin Reader Service, P.O. Box 1341, Buffalo, NY 14240-8531 or visit www.ReaderService.com ▲

BUSINESS REPLY MAIL
FIRST-CLASS MAIL   PERMIT NO. 717   BUFFALO, NY

POSTAGE WILL BE PAID BY ADDRESSEE

HARLEQUIN READER SERVICE
PO BOX 1341
BUFFALO NY 14240-8571

NO POSTAGE
NECESSARY
IF MAILED
IN THE
UNITED STATES

pect stopped and gulped. "I shouldn't be talking, but my mind's a mess right now."

Probably the reason she hadn't thought to ask for legal counsel before speaking, but Rylan wasn't about to remind her of her rights when she'd had them recited to her more than once already.

"What did Dennis Dorfman say?" Rylan's tone demanded an immediate answer.

Leota leaned toward him, a furtive look on her face, as if they were coconspirators. "We were in Denver when it happened, Double D and I. But afterward, you know, one of the shooters told Double D, who told me, about a 'big mistake'—" she bracketed the two words in finger quotation marks "—in Wyoming, and they had to make a body and some other stuff disappear. That's it. That's all. Can I have my methadone now?"

Rylan's gaze swung toward the one-way glass. Now they had independent confirmation—albeit via hearsay— that a murder had truly taken place in Burling. How did Emily feel about that revelation? Validated? Or more terrified than ever?

NINE

Emily sat cuddling Oliver in Annie's living room after breakfast the morning following the chaotic ambush at the motel complex. She and Oliver were home alone since Annie had gone to work, but the house was under surveillance, and new security systems had been installed on all windows and doors. They were safe enough—certainly safer than during yesterday's risky operation.

She should be feeling relieved that her role as bait was over and had gotten results, but Emily's insides were strung as taut as bowstrings. Oliver seemed to be feeding off her tension, as he was restless and fussy. She felt his forehead and didn't detect a fever, and he had no other symptoms like a runny nose, cough or colic. No, he had to be sensing her inner turmoil, and for his sake, she needed to get her mind and emotions right. Easier said than done.

Was she a military wife—or widow—as her dream had suggested?

Had she been confined to bed during the latter part of her pregnancy?

How literally should she take the dream? In the moment, it had seemed so real—a factual representation of past reality. Second-guessing had kept her from sharing the contents of the dream with Sheriff Pierce yesterday. With the new leads from Leota, a suspect to interview in the hospital, forensic evidence to evaluate and an investigation of the drug link to Denver, the man had too much on his plate already. But a tidbit like she'd been married to a serviceman might be helpful. Then again, if her subconscious was playing tricks on her, throwing a mistaken detail into the mix could only add confusion and lead to nothing.

But what if her dream-memory led to *something*? She couldn't simply ignore information her damaged psyche might be smuggling to her in a dream. The next chance she got, she was going to tell all to Rylan. With that decision made, the interior turmoil eased, and she settled onto a blanket on the floor to play with Oliver. He was soon giggling, and she laughed along with his innocent pleasure at peekaboo. Nothing like sweet, harmless fun to drive the problems away—at least temporarily.

The buzz of a cell phone lying atop the nearby coffee table halted the laughter in Emily's throat. She glanced at the instrument vibrating against the glass top. Rylan had given her the pay-as-you-go phone before escorting her to Annie's house last evening and told her his personal cell number was the only one programmed in it, and he alone had her number.

Gingerly, she took the phone in her hand and keyed the screen to answer.

"Hello?"

"It's me," the sheriff's voice responded. "How are you and Oliver doing this morning?"

Emily's heart warmed that the sheriff had made time for small talk with her. Then again, maybe the inquiry wasn't merely casual conversation. Her well-being and that of Oliver had been the main focus of his department for many days now.

"We're good. Thanks to Drover's Creek's finest and the kind folk of the town chipping in to supply us."

Rylan's deep chuckle brought a smile to her face.

"How's the investigation going?"

"Fits and starts." His tone sobered. "We've confirmed Dennis Dorfman as a small-time drug dealer from Colorado."

"It strikes me as odd that the people attacking me have devolved from guys who seem like pros to a motley crew of minor crooks."

"You're sharp, as always. I suspect whoever is running this show might be experiencing personnel challenges since we chased off the man-mountain who came after you in the hospital, as well as the eight guys in the SUVs who tried to cut us off near the original safe house. We've got descriptions for all these goons and would recognize them around town. So they had to scrounge up lowlifes from somewhere who were willing to do the tasks. One thing Mr. Mastermind isn't short on, however, is tech toys. Leota used a top-of-the-line snap gun to pick the door lock in a split second. We recovered it from the floor of the cabin, with her prints all over it."

Emily let out a long hum. "I guess that leaves the

question of who spotted me at the motel complex and let the pinch-hitting crew know my location."

"Yeah, that bothers me. A lot. We didn't see the ones who attacked you at the cabin lurking around town, watching. They had to have been in hiding until they were called upon to move in. Whoever had eyes on you was either a known individual in this town—an option that curdles my stomach—or maybe using more of the gadgetry this guy seems to like."

"Hacking into surveillance cameras around town, maybe?"

Rylan chuckled. "In a quiet, backwater burg like Drover's Creek, those are few and far between, though the gas station next door to the motel has a couple— one inside the convenience store and one focused on the gas pumps. Neither of them would have picked up your arrival at the motel."

"How about drones, then?"

Silence fell for a couple of beats. "You might have an idea, there. Those things are getting more sophisticated all the time. We'll put the word out in town to watch for any flying around and report sightings."

"I have a couple of thoughts on another area of this situation." Emily gulped in a steadying breath. She was committed now to telling him her dream. "When you get a minute, could you come over here? I'd like to have an in-person discussion. Maybe you could drop in for lunch? I'll cook."

"Can't turn down an offer like that. Besides, I'm always ready to hear your thoughts. We need all the help we can get to figure out this mess."

After a few more words of casual conversation, they

ended the call. Emily got up, leaving Oliver with his toys, and went to the kitchen to see what Annie might have in stock to fix for a noon meal. The older woman had told her to help herself to any supplies she found.

As she browsed the cupboards, the freezer and the refrigerator, meal ideas popped into her head, as well as exactly how to cook them. And not just meal ideas. A bar recipe floated full-blown and unbidden into her consciousness. Apparently, she liked to cook and bake. Who knew?

By the time Rylan arrived at the house, Emily had shrimp scampi with linguini and a side salad with a homemade dressing prepared, and a pan of bars were baking in the oven. The sheriff walked into the kitchen and inhaled deeply.

"Wow!"

Emily beamed at the reaction, and he grinned. Oxygen turned to helium in her lungs. If the air became any more electric, breakers would trip. Then Rylan cleared his throat, his gaze tore away from hers and he looked toward the small table set with country ceramic plates and simple cutlery.

"Thanks for inviting me over. By the savory smell of things around here, you could give Barb competition."

Emily shook her head and dished scampi onto the plates. "No, I think our cooking styles differ quite a bit. Country-compared-to-metro kind of thing. So let's call it complementation."

"Apparently, you've remembered a skill set." He took a seat at the table. "Anything else come to mind?"

"That's what I want to talk to you about but not until

we've eaten. Oliver just went down for a nap, so we should be uninterrupted."

Rylan shot her a sharp look, but Emily forced herself to ignore the unspoken prompt for answers and took the seat across from him.

"I see you're no longer wearing a bandage on your head."

Involuntarily, her fingers went to her temple, where a long strand of hair covered the shaved area around the sutured head wound. The light touch sent a twinge of discomfort through her, but the pain was already less than yesterday.

"After seeing to the addicted woman at your jail last night, Doc Laura dropped by here and checked me out. Said I didn't need to cover the wound anymore, and I'm glad to have the bandage off."

"You look nice."

Emily's cheeks warmed, and she ducked her head.

Rylan cleared his throat and offered a short prayer of thanksgiving. Then they dug into the food. Conversation remained light as they ate. At last, they sat back with coffee cups in one hand and warm bars in the other.

"What have you got for me?" Rylan's steady stare tolerated no more delay.

Emily put her bar down on the plate as the bite on her tongue turned to sawdust. Haltingly at first and then rapidly, she recounted her dream to the sheriff, and he allowed her to finish without question or comment.

He popped the last of a second bar into his mouth, wiped his fingers on a napkin and set the crumpled paper down next to his plate. "Let me see if I get this right. Your dream suggests you may have been married to a serviceman and received a death notification at a time when you were in the midst of a high-risk pregnancy?"

Emily nodded wordlessly, her insides tied in knots. Were the details of the grievous situation what her waking mind so desperately refused to recall?

The sheriff's face settled into solemn planes, and his hand slid across the table to cover one of hers. "If the tragic news threw you into labor, that scenario could suggest an emergency C-section."

Emily closed her fingers around his as if clinging to a lifeline. "Exactly. I don't consciously *know* the elements of my dream are true, but I *feel* they are. Will this information help you find out who I am?"

"It will narrow some parameters. Do you remember any details about the uniforms? Color, perhaps?"

She shook her head. "The dream was all sepia-toned."

"How about any patches or medals?"

"Those things were a blur. Nothing stood out."

"All right, then. I can reach out to the military community. I have contacts. But no guarantees. We'll do our best—that, I can promise you."

"I trust your promise."

For long seconds, they sat there, hands entwined. Then a ringtone sounded from the sheriff's shirt pocket. Emily pulled her hand back, face heating, and Rylan plucked out the phone. He answered brusquely, as if his throat was thick.

Someone on the other end—Annie?—spoke a few terse sentences. Emily couldn't make out the words, but the sheriff suddenly stiffened.

"Tell them I'll be right there."

He ended the call and stared across the table at her. Emily shifted in her seat. What had happened to leach the color out of Rylan's face?

"Last night, I touched base again with the marshals service to let them know we have verbal confirmation that a murder occurred in Burling, and it's reasonable to suppose you witnessed it. Now there's a pair of federal deputies at my headquarters, waiting to take you and Oliver into protective custody."

Emily's mouth dropped open. Leave Drover's Creek? Even though she and Oliver had been under constant attack here, the sheriff and his crew had become her safety net and the generous people of the community her welcoming haven. Going with the deputy marshals meant trusting herself to strangers. A chill gripped her limbs. Worse. It meant not seeing Rylan again—maybe ever. Something shriveled deep inside her.

Rylan pocketed his cell phone. His chest had gone vacant, as if his heart had fallen out and onto the floor. Emily and Oliver were *his* to protect. Or, rather, this county's law enforcement's responsibility. Though if he was honest with himself, the first knee-jerk thought was truer to what was going on inside him. Yet the federal agency undoubtedly had a deeper infrastructure to ensure Emily and Oliver's safety, as well as to dig for the truth behind what was going on. However, he was going to vet these deputies thoroughly and clarify the intentions of the marshals service toward his charges and their case.

"Stay here," he told Emily. "I want to go talk to the deputies and touch base with their office. After Oliver wakes up, call the department, and someone will come to walk you over to headquarters."

Emily nodded wordlessly, and he studied her pale countenance. Maybe it would be best for her and Oliver to go with the deputies. Maybe she *wanted* to go with them after all the attacks she'd experienced here in Drover's Creek.

"Thank you for the excellent lunch and the new leads." He stood up. "If the feds take over, they might be able to run with your information better than I can."

She offered a tremulous smile. "You're welcome. About the meal, I mean. My pleasure. It seemed the least I could do, but—" Her flurry of words came to a halt. "Now I'm babbling. What I'd really like to say is I have mixed feelings about going with the deputies, though your people and this community might breathe a sigh of relief to see the backs of us."

"Don't even think such a thing!" The passion in his words surprised even himself. "Make no mistake," he continued in a more measured tone, "the staff in my office have practically adopted you and Oliver, and the people of Drover's Creek are rooting for you. We'd all feel the loss if you went."

"Thank you." Her gaze lightened, and she beamed up at him. "That sentiment means the world to this anchorless soul."

With a nod, he turned and left the house. On the way across the street, his mind churned over the case. Even with the testimony gleaned from Leota and the hints contained in Emily's dream, the facts were thin and clues nebulous. Why then would the marshals service send people out of the blue to collect Oliver and Emily so quickly after he'd updated them with sparse details? Then again, maybe something he didn't know about the case had lit a fire under them. If so, he'd appreciate them telling him what that was. He wasn't going to allow them to swoop in here and snatch up his charges without a word of explanation.

Rylan let himself in through the rear entrance and found the bullpen moderately busy, but no strangers were present.

"Where are our federal guests?" he asked no one in particular but everyone all at once.

Steve pointed toward the front entry and dispatch area.

Rylan frowned. "No one invited them back here?"

"Annie offered to let them wait in your office, complete with coffee and a couple of Barb's cinnamon rolls, but they declined. Their loss. They seem in a bit of a hurry."

A soft snort left Rylan's lips. Hurry? Not until explanations were forthcoming.

He strode through the door into the dispatcher's station. From her seat behind the glassed-in window, Annie scowled at him. Clearly she was unimpressed by their federal guests, but maybe that was because, like him, she didn't want to see Emily and Oliver go. Rylan answered her with an infinitesimal shake of the head. This was not about liking the situation. They would do whatever was right.

He switched his gaze toward the waiting area beyond the glass. A pair of dark-suited, shiny-shoed deputies sat, sober-faced and anything but relaxed, on the metal-and-plastic chairs that lined the far wall. At Rylan's appearance, the male and female deputies rose and stepped forward in lockstep. The female was short and sturdy, with a full-moon face; the male was tall and lanky, with sharp features. They both flipped open their ID cases, displaying their star badges and a card bearing printed details.

"Deputies Carstairs and Delgado," Rylan read aloud. Then he motioned toward them and opened the locked metal door that separated the waiting area from the rest of the building. "Come on back to my office. We need to talk."

The pair frowned at each other but walked through the doorway.

"Sheriff Pierce, we'd like to get our charges to the safe house as quickly as possible," said the female deputy identified as Carstairs.

"Let's discuss that." Rylan strode away, forcing them to follow him across the bullpen and into the sanctity of his space. "Wait here." He gestured at the sofa. "I'll get us some coffee."

"No, thanks," the deputies practically chorused.

"Tea, then?"

"Nothing for us. Thank you," Carstairs said firmly, her ice-blue gaze bordering on feral.

"Well, I want something." Rylan tendered a benign smile and left the room, drawing the door shut behind him. He moved quickly to Steve's workstation. "Call the Wyoming Marshals Service office and verify they sent these two deputies here. They arrived awfully fast. Federal bureaucracy usually grinds along slower."

"You think the deputies are bogus?"

"Not really. They have the right credentials, and they

look and act the part. There's just something… I don't know. Maybe I'm being overly cautious."

"No such thing in our occupation." Steve picked up the receiver of the landline phone on the corner of his desk.

Rylan went and got a cup of the coffee he'd claimed to want and then returned to his office. The deputies hadn't taken advantage of the seating he'd offered. They were still on their feet.

"You might as well take a load off. We're a small department with a big territory. Not much happens in a hurry here."

With frowns and glances toward each other, the pair sat—the male on the sofa, the female in the guest chair. Rylan settled into the seat behind his desk, sat back and took a sip of his coffee.

"Tell me what spurred the marshals service to want to take over this case?"

The pair exchanged glances again. The mannerism was beginning to irritate Rylan.

Delgado cleared his throat. "We would think you'd be pleased to offload this mess onto a department equipped to handle a major threat coming from someone who appears to possess intimidating resources."

"I have all the respect in the world for the marshals service, but you didn't answer my question."

Delgado shrugged. "We don't have the answer. Our orders come from higher up."

Rylan frowned into his coffee. The old *we're just doing what we're told* brush-off. Yet the claim of ignorance could well be true—possibly even likely.

Steve appeared in his doorway and gave him a thumbs-up. Rylan bottled a sigh. The legitimate presence of these deputies was confirmed. He had no choice but to produce Emily and Oliver.

He nodded toward Steve. "Send Sarah over to see if Oliver is up from his nap and, if so, to escort our charges here."

"Will do." Steve withdrew.

"Tell me, then," Rylan said to his federal guests, "what is meant by 'protective custody' in this case? The only identified suspects so far are low-level drug dealers. Surely the marshals service isn't offering the full-blown witness protection program to Emily in order to keep her safe so she can testify against them in court."

"You are correct," Carstairs said. "We won't be enrolling Ms. Doe—er, Emily—and the baby in WITSEC at this stage, though it is a possibility, depending on who is identified as being behind the murder Ms. Doe witnessed and the subsequent attacks on her."

"I take it, since you're acknowledging her as a Jane Doe, you realize she has no clear memory of the murder. How would that work on the witness stand?"

Delgado offered a grin about as warm as a barracuda's. "In our custody, she will be placed under the care of a psychiatrist, who can hopefully help her retrieve her memories."

"That sounds all fine and good." Rylan gave himself a mental kick for not seeing to it that Emily received psychiatric care before now, but events had seemed to pile on top of each other, not leaving much downtime.

Steve appeared in Rylan's doorway. "They're here."

Rylan rose and stepped around his desk, but the pair of federal deputies beat him out the door in a rush that saw them nearly collide. Shaking his head, Rylan stepped out into the bullpen to find Emily standing in the middle of the room with Oliver in her arms. The small, wheeled case she'd used for the trap yesterday and Oliver's diaper bag sat at her feet. Her slump-shouldered posture and the slight sway as she distributed her weight from one foot to another broadcasted uncertainty.

Rylan met Emily's gaze with what he hoped was a reassuring smile. Her attention flitted toward the pair of federal deputies.

She shook her head. "We can't go."

The deputies' bodies went rigid.

"Ollie doesn't have a car seat," Emily went on. "It was in the wrecked van from yesterday."

Carstairs's posture relaxed. "No worries. We've got one in our car."

Rylan frowned. Not only had these deputies showed up fast, but they also took bureaucratic preparation to an unusually thorough level. His gut tensed. Everything checked out about their presence, but something didn't smell right.

"Let's go." Delgado led the way out of the bullpen, through the dispatcher's station and into the waiting area. Emily and Oliver were ushered along between the deputies.

Rylan took up the rear of the procession, studying the deputies' demeanors. Beyond tense. Definitely too eager to depart. He might be overreacting but... His fingers slid to the holster at his waist and fingered the snap of the catch that held his weapon in place.

In the reception area, Emily came to a halt. Her gaze went from Rylan to Annie and then to the pair of deputy marshals.

Finally, she fixed her attention on Rylan. "Do I have a choice?"

His heart leaped. "You're not under arrest, so you certainly do."

A smile bloomed on her face as certainty settled over her expression. "Then I'm not leaving. I'm going to stay right here."

Delgado's professional mask shattered into a teeth-bared snarl. "You're coming with us."

He reached for Emily's arm, but she pulled away, only to be grabbed by Carstairs and dragged toward the door. Emily screamed. Oliver wailed. Delgado reached under his suit toward his shoulder holster, but Rylan took his hand off his weapon. He couldn't have bullets flying near the baby.

Instead, he charged the fake deputy, who was reaching for his gun. Rylan was many years past achieving his tackling record in high school football, but he'd never lost his muscle tone and—*Please, God!*—his speed might still be enough.

TEN

Emily yanked against the iron fingers gripping her upper arm, but the attempt to break free while maintaining her two-armed protective embrace around a wailing, squirming Oliver proved awkward. Also, the federal deputy apparently possessed tremendous strength. As the sheriff lunged toward the other deputy, Emily found herself dragged backward through the front door of the law enforcement headquarters building and onto the sidewalk lining the busy downtown street.

She winced against the sudden onslaught of bright sunshine and dry heat, as well as the band of pressure pinching her arm. In a change of tactic, Emily stopped fighting the deputy's grip and leaned into it. The woman staggered, snarling a foul word, but maintained her hold.

At the strange sight, several nearby townspeople froze in their tracks and stared.

"Help us!" Emily cried out, kicking against her captor's leg.

Her foot rammed the deputy's shin, and the woman cried out. The grip on Emily's arm went away, only to be replaced with both arms wrapping around Emily and Oliver, crushing them to the deputy's chest. Lifting them from the ground, the woman limped with her burden closer to a dark sedan parked at the curb.

Shouting and the sounds of fists meeting flesh sounded from within the law enforcement building. Was Rylan taking down the other federal deputy? As she struggled against the arms locked around her, Emily's gaze sought to discover what might be happening, but the brick wall and darkened glass denied her any information.

"Let them go," demanded an onlooker—a burly, middle-aged man in a worn shirt and jeans, cowboy hat, and cowboy boots. The man strode closer, fists bunching.

"Do not interfere." The deputy's voice emerged in a commanding growl. "I'm a US deputy marshal. These people are coming with me."

"We're not." Emily kicked again, and the woman stumbled back against the rear side panel of the unmarked marshals service vehicle.

Odd banging noises came from the trunk, but Emily had no spare time to ponder the strange phenomenon as more townspeople crowded closer, some of them rushing in from across the street. Men and women, most of them in casual clothes but one or two in suits, enclosed them in a semicircle to their fore with the sedan at their rear. The deputy's hot breath panted in Emily's ear like a cornered and desperate animal.

A large woman wearing a flour-dusted apron over jeans and a T-shirt folded her arms across an ample bosom and glared. "You're not taking our Emily and Ollie anywhere."

"Barb is correct," said a familiar voice, and Emily's heart leaped.

Sheriff Rylan shouldered his way to the front of the crowd, his gray gaze like steel arrows aimed at the woman holding Emily and Oliver in an octopus grip.

"We've got your partner in custody, and you have no way of escape," the sheriff said, the icy calm in his tone more threatening than any shout. "Give it up."

With a sound like a mix of a whine and a snarl, the female deputy released Emily. Her feet hit the cement, and she staggered forward. Welcoming arms swept her and a whimpering Oliver into a protective circle of townspeople. Emily's head swam. She inhaled the first deep breath she'd taken since the ordeal began, and equilibrium returned. Patting her baby's back, she cooed to him, and he settled, gazing around at the people with wide, curious eyes. Faces beamed at him, and he responded with a smile.

More law enforcement personnel streamed outside, with Sarah, Steve and Big Dave among them. A hush fell over the area as the police chief took custody of the now-cuffed deputy marshal. The prisoner's face was bright red, as if she could combust at any moment, but she said nothing. Emily's gaze followed the woman as Big Dave perp-walked her into the headquarters building.

The banging in the trunk of the marshals service sedan became pronounced, along with muffled cries from within. The sheriff's puzzled gaze met Emily's. Evidently, the male deputy marshal must have gotten a lick in, because his left cheekbone sported a red mark that promised to become a bruise.

"Are you okay?" he asked.

"We're doing well, thanks to your department and these fine people. Whoever's in the trunk might not be in such good shape."

Rylan frowned and motioned toward Sarah. "Don't let any surprises pop out of here when I hit the trunk release."

"I'm on it." The officer unsnapped her holster and her hand rested on the butt of her service weapon, though she didn't yet draw it. Her gaze fixed on the vehicle's rear.

The sheriff headed for the driver's side of the sedan. Apparently, the vehicle wasn't locked, because he opened the door without a hitch and reached inside. A latch *thunked*, and the trunk lid popped ajar but remained mostly down. The interior of the trunk went silent.

As if of one mind, the crowd surged forward, with Emily caught in the scrum, but the sheriff shooed everyone back.

"Keep your distance. We don't know what we're going to find."

"I have a suspicion," Emily said.

Rylan offered her a lopsided smile. "Me too, but we'll err on the side of caution."

He nodded toward Sarah. The officer drew her weapon and trained it on the back end of the vehicle. Standing clear to one side, Rylan lifted the trunk lid. Two sets of angry eyes above taped-shut mouths and bound limbs glared out at everyone.

The sheriff let out a long, loud sigh. "I think we've found the *real* deputy marshals." He gazed around at the townspeople. "I'm very proud of all of you. It's my honor to serve this community. But the excitement's over, and it's time now for everyone to go about their own business. I have no doubt the robust local grapevine will keep the whole county informed of breaking events." He grinned.

The people grinned back, and many of them waved as they moved away, conversations already buzzing between them. Emily smiled. The grapevine was about to flare red hot.

"Sarah, Steve," Rylan called out. "See about releasing our fellow law enforcement personnel and getting them comfortable inside."

The sheriff stepped up onto the sidewalk and put an arm around Emily's shoulders. The warm touch broke through a protective shell and set off a reaction, and she began to shiver despite the desert heat.

"Let's get you tucked away in my office." The sheriff squeezed her close.

She allowed him to shepherd her through the door into the front entry. Her gaze studied his stony profile. Annie offered a few words of comfort and affirmation as they made their way through her area. Emily acknowledged the caring with a nod and a tremulous smile, but Rylan stared straight ahead.

Moments later, he gently settled her and Oliver on his sofa, shut his office door and plopped into his desk chair. Both hands lay before him on the desktop, balled into fists, though the bandages still wrapping his left hand restricted the movement somewhat. The hot glare he fixed at a nebulous spot in the ether could have boiled water.

Emily cleared her throat. "I get you're angry about

the attempted abduction—but once again, this law enforcement team and this community came through for Ollie and me. You should be proud and relieved."

Rylan's expression softened, and he met her gaze. "The situation shouldn't have been a near miss. I messed up big-time."

"How?"

"I sensed something off about the fake deputies right away. Sure, they looked the part—even had the cop vibe—but I didn't notice when they showed me their IDs that their thumbs mostly covered their photos. Rookie mistake." He rubbed the forming bruise on his cheek.

"Who expects you to be perfect? At least you weren't one of those deputy marshals who wound up in a trunk with their identifications stolen. Now, *there's* a situation they might find hard to explain to their superiors."

"I *am* the superior in this office, and I let everyone down, especially you and Oliver." Rylan turned his wounded eyes on Emily. "Maybe you *should* take advantage of federal custody."

Emily set her jaw. "I told you I'm not going anywhere, and I meant it."

"But what if I fail you and Oliver?" His tone emerged in a harsh whisper.

"But what if you don't?" Her firm pronouncement belied the hideous flickers of disaster scenarios lurking in the back of her mind.

Whatever the future held, sticking with people who had a proven track record of caring for her and Oliver, and coming out on top of every situation, simply seemed to be the wisest course. A formidable array of personnel and an arsenal of technical resources hadn't defeated Rylan and his team yet.

Still, the enemy only had to get it right once for her to be dead and Oliver gone. She and Rylan and the law enforcement community of Buck County and Drover's Creek needed to figure out what was going on before that happened. If only she could coax her mind to give up the knowledge necessary to put a stop to the relentless attacks.

Rylan stared into the eyes of the woman whom he'd come to highly respect and esteem. He might not know her real name any more than she did, but he knew her character. What she was made of had been tested under fire before his very eyes multiple times. Everything about her appealed to him, and that's what scared him. Once her memory returned, and the evil that pursued her and Oliver had been thwarted, she'd leave Buck County and resume her life. And he would let her even if his heart tore in two. She deserved every bit of happiness and peace she could find.

"I know you must have a thousand things to do," Emily said. "But would you mind holding Oliver for a few minutes? I'd like to freshen up in the bathroom."

Rylan mentally shook himself and reached out his arms to receive the baby. "I've got a few minutes until the fake deputies are booked into our system and ready for interviews, so I don't mind a bit getting better acquainted with this sturdy fellow."

Oliver came onto his lap without a squawk and was immediately fascinated with his sheriff's badge and nameplate.

"Take all the time you need. If something comes up that demands my handling, there are lots of folks around here who would gladly take over with him."

With a quick thank-you, she left the room.

Rylan looked down into Oliver's eyes, and the little guy offered a winsome, toothless grin. Rylan grinned back, searching his memory for things he'd seen other people do to entertain small children. Lifting the baby, he let the infant stand on his lap. Oliver immediately grabbed Rylan's nose, and Rylan spurted out a raspberry onto the baby's tiny palm and wrist. The child let out a chortle and pulled his hand back. Rylan hefted the baby and blew another raspberry onto his round, little tummy. Cackles filled the room, and Rylan couldn't help laughing along with Oliver. Just like that, whatever gloom that remained on his heart was thoroughly dispelled.

Minutes passed in innocent play, and Rylan realized something: kids were the world's greatest attitude adjusters. Adults got bogged down with worries and responsibilities and soon could no longer see the sunny meadow for the dismal swamp. Basking in the carefree happiness of a small child restored perspective, something he badly needed at the moment.

Raised voices in the bullpen intruded on Rylan's epiphany. One of those voices was Emily's. Playtime was over. Rylan gathered Oliver to his chest with one arm and headed out his door. The real male and female deputy marshals, looking none the worse for wear, were confronting Emily. All three figures held themselves rigid, and the atmosphere in the bullpen had gone electric.

"What's going on out here?" Rylan demanded.

Emily's head swiveled toward him. "These two—" she jerked her thumb toward the federal deputies "—still think Oliver and I should come with them. But I'm not going."

Frowning, the female deputy—the real Carstairs— turned toward Rylan. Except for her hair color, the woman didn't much resemble her impersonator. This person was willowy and fine-featured.

"Our assignment was to take the two subjects into protective custody," she said. "The assignment hasn't changed."

"Quite a lot has changed." Rylan handed Oliver off to his mother. "Come into my office, and we'll place a call to your superior together."

The federal pair shifted their weight from one foot to the other and exchanged glances. The male deputy didn't look much like his impostor, either. He was roughly the same height as the suspect in custody, but this guy was beefy with muscle, and his face was craggy and rough. The lack of substantial resemblance between the real deputies and the fake had necessitated the fake ones to hold their thumbs over the ID photos. It would be a long time before Rylan forgave himself for overlooking that breach of identification protocol and coming so close to having Emily and Oliver abducted from under his nose.

"I take it you haven't called this incident in yet." Rylan's sentence came out as a statement rather than a question.

Clearly the deputy marshals were trying to salvage the situation for themselves by showing up successfully at their end with their charges before admitting they'd been waylaid and impersonated. But the two feds were in the Buck County patch now, and Rylan wasn't about to let that maneuver fly.

He settled a gentle gaze on Emily. "I've got this. Hang out with Annie if you'd like, before I get someone shaken loose around here to escort you back to her place."

Emily's gaze darted between him and the two scowling federal deputies. Then she jerked a nod and walked off in the direction of the dispatcher area.

Rylan motioned toward Delgado and Carstairs. The pair followed him with expressions like they'd been sucking on lemons and postures as if they were being summoned into the principal's office. They all settled into seats in the sheriff's office—Carstairs on the sofa, Delgado in the guest chair and Rylan in his own familiar desk chair.

"Go ahead and make the call. You can use my landline—" Rylan gestured toward the cordless extension on the corner of his desk "—or your cell phone. Either way, we'll put it on speaker."

"What is the status of the two suspects who ambushed us?" asked Delgado.

"They're in a holding cell by now, I would imagine. We'll get to them in due course…and I think you'll like my idea of what to do with them." Rylan offered each of the deputies a collegial smile.

They exchanged glances, a mannerism they shared with their impersonators, and some of the starch went out of their spines. Carstairs pulled out a phone and tapped in a number. The phone rang twice.

"Marshal Tucker here." The female voice was brisk and no-nonsense.

Goose bumps ran up and down Rylan's arms. He'd expected the phone to be answered by a supervisory deputy US marshal, not by the presidentially appointed head honcho for the entire district. As he'd speculated, the feds knew or suspected something big was behind whatever was going on with Emily and Oliver.

"Carstairs," the marshal continued, "you and your partner should be on your way to Cheyenne from Drover's Creek by now. Tell me you have secured the subjects."

"Er, no. We're sitting in the Buck County sheriff's office."

"Is Sheriff Pierce being obstructive?"

"No, he is not," Rylan said. "Things got complicated."

"Ah, Sheriff Pierce. I take it we are on speakerphone."

"Just Rylan, please."

"Very well, Rylan. Complicated how?"

"I'll let your people fill you in."

Delgado cleared his throat. "Someone knew we were on our way to Drover's Creek from the branch office in Lander. About halfway here, we stopped at a convenience store and were ambushed by individuals with Tasers. Then we were injected with some sort of knockout drug. We woke up in the trunk of our sedan in Drover's Creek with an altercation happening outside the vehicle."

Silence fell for several heartbeats.

"Were shots fired?" the marshal asked.

"Negative," Rylan said. "Physical confrontation ended with the arrest of two suspects impersonating your deputies. Emily and Oliver are unharmed."

"Emily and Oliver?"

"The names we've given to the individuals your people intended to collect. As you are aware, Emily's memory has been affected by a severe concussion coupled with the trauma she experienced in witnessing a murder—at least, that last part is the current medical opinion. We haven't had a chance to get her seen by an expert in the psychiatric field."

The marshal hummed. "We can see to that on our end when she arrives."

"Marshal Tucker, ma'am," Carstairs said, "Ms. Doe is refusing our protective custody."

"You've got to be kidding me!" If steam could pour through a cell phone connection, Rylan wouldn't have been surprised to witness the manifestation. "Then again, after what just occurred in Drover's Creek, one could hardly blame her for lack of trust. Put her on for me, will you, please?"

"Hang on a minute." Rylan got up, went to his door and poked his head out while the marshal inquired about her deputies' health after their ordeal. Rylan motioned to Steve and told him to ask Emily to come to his office. In a moment, she emerged from the dispatcher's area and stepped tentatively across the room toward him. Her arms were empty. Evidently, she'd left Oliver with Annie.

"It's going to be all right." Rylan hastened to reassure her as he ushered her into his office. "The District US Marshal wants to speak with you."

Emily stood beside him, eyeing the lit cell phone on his desk like it might be a trap. "Hello?" she said, a slight tremor in her voice.

"Ms. Doe—er, Emily," the marshal said. "This is Vivienne Tucker. As Sheriff Pierce told you, I'm the district marshal. We'd like to offer you and your baby our assistance and protection. Despite the rocky start between you and my department, we really are your best hope of remaining safe until this matter is resolved."

"I disagree." All uncertainty had left Emily's tone. "Sheriff Rylan, his department, the city police and the community of Drover's Creek have stood like a wall between Ollie and me and anyone who would try to harm us. I won't feel safe anywhere else."

"I know you think that way at the moment, Emily, but—"

"Allow me to suggest an alternate possibility."

Rylan's interruption drew an irritated hiss from the marshal.

"Go ahead." The words emerged in a grudging tone.

"We here in Buck County will continue to look after Emily and Oliver. But your people are more than welcome to take custody of the suspects involved in the assault on your deputies and the attempted kidnapping of this woman and her baby. Your department has resources mine does not for finding out these yahoos' identities and who is giving them orders. I have only one stipulation—or *request* might be the better way of putting it."

"What is that?"

"In order to best protect Emily and Oliver, my office needs to know right now what you know or what you even suspect, and we need to be kept up-to-date on what you find out."

"To me, that sounds like two requests."

"Think of it as two halves of one whole."

The marshal chuckled. "Nicely done, Sheriff Pierce... Rylan. We'll gladly take the deputy impersonators off your hands, but I already have an idea as to who they are. Tell me, is the female a short, stocky Caucasian and the male a tall, lanky Hispanic?"

"Affirmative," Delgado put in.

The Marshal sighed. "If they are whom I suspect, they are disgraced ex-cops who are known associates of a federal fugitive we've been after for almost a decade. Why precisely this fugitive has poked his head out of hiding to go after your Emily and Oliver, we are not sure. It has to be more than her witnessing a crime. What we do know is that this man's son was recently killed in a shoot-out with ATF agents in Denver, Colorado. As a result, we had been waiting for—no, hoping for—a reaction from the father that might lead us to him."

Rylan's eyebrows climbed toward his hairline. "The Bureau of Alcohol, Tobacco, Firearms and Explosives? How are they involved? Was this guy's son an arms trafficker?"

"Arms *and* drugs, one-upping his parent. Ward Spencer, the deceased male's father, was once the biggest illegal arms distributor in the western half of the United States. He was arrested, convicted and sent to prison for what amounts to the rest of his natural life. But nine and a half years ago, he escaped prison and has been a wanted fugitive ever since. Much of this criminal's assets were never found or confiscated, so we assumed that his money purchased him a lavish lifestyle in some non-extradition country. And maybe he had indeed fled the United States, but now it seems he's back, and we intend to catch him."

A tremor passed through Rylan. The sort of guy the marshal described certainly had access to the kinds of resources they seemed to be up against. Then a question occurred to him.

"Is there any link between this arms dealer and an LLC named Centaur Financial Group?"

"Let me check the case file online." The ensuing silence was punctuated with keyboard clacks and a pair of soft hums from the marshal. "Centaur Financial Group is listed among entities suspected of laundering money for the Spencers, father *and* son. How did you know about this company?"

Rylan filled the woman in about the thugs who showed up in town driving vehicles rented through the LLC. "Your information nicely ties up a loose end for us and provides another evidentiary link to the arms dealer."

A small hand gripped Rylan's arm, and he looked down to find Emily gazing up at him with a pale face and wide eyes.

"This Ward Spencer—how dangerous is he?"

Rylan opened his mouth, but no answer emerged. He'd give anything to have a reassuring answer to offer, but the nature of this guy's business and the scope of it signaled he had to be among the worst of the ruthless.

"Honestly?" Marshal Tucker said. "A coiled rattler would be easier to handle."

ELEVEN

Emily inhaled a deep, shaky breath and let it out slowly. "Thank you for your candor, Marshal Tucker. No disrespect toward the marshals service, but my answer remains the same. I'm staying here in Drover's Creek."

Rylan's warm hand covered hers on his arm, but the welcome touch fell away almost immediately. Emily released his arm and stepped back from him. Clingy behavior went against every instinct inside her. Plus, she hadn't the emotional energy to confront what she might be starting to feel for the sheriff outside of his official capacity.

"Very well," said the marshal. "My deputies will take custody of the suspects apprehended today, and you and your baby will remain in the care of Buck County. But, Sheriff Rylan, I expect regular updates and transparency from your department."

"You've got it," Rylan said. "*Mutual* updates."

The marshal chuckled. "It's a pleasure dealing with you, Sheriff. Carstairs, Delgado, I'll expect you in Cheyenne with the suspects tomorrow. It's too late this afternoon to head this way. Get some rest and have yourselves looked at by a doctor after your experience."

Delgado grimaced. "I'm fine, ma'am."

Carstairs socked her partner on the arm. "Stop being such a *guy*. We'll get checked out by a doctor, ma'am. Don't worry. See you tomorrow."

Silence fell, but no one disconnected the call.

"Shall we address the elephant in the room?" the marshal asked.

Rylan frowned, and Emily's heart sank. What was wrong now? Well, besides deadly and determined people mounting repeated attacks at the behest of a vicious gunrunner.

The sheriff crossed his arms over his chest. "How did Spencer find out about your deputies' mission in time to mount an interception?"

"Yes, that's the elephant," the marshal agreed.

"All I can say to that is this office was unaware of your bureau's intentions until the deputies showed up here."

The marshal muttered something angrily under her breath. "My apologies. We dropped the ball on notifying you of our decision to take custody prior to the deputies' arrival."

"When was that decision made?"

"Shortly after you called last night. Within the hour of that decision, you should have received an email and a phone call regarding our intentions."

"Who was in charge of the communication?"

"My personal assistant, who texted this morning to say she was not feeling well and wouldn't be coming in. The matter will be immediately investigated."

Emily scanned the faces of the law enforcement personnel around her. The illness must be spreading. They all looked as sick as the marshal sounded and the assistant claimed to be. One question remained: Had someone forced the assistant to divulge the information, or did the marshals service have a mole in its midst?

"I'll leave you to your investigation, then, Marshal Tucker."

"I'll be in touch." The woman's tone had turned to steel. No one liked discovering a fatal flaw in their operations.

The call ended, and Emily's shoulders drooped. If her enemy could reach inside federal law enforcement and pluck out information, how could she expect *anyone* to protect her and Oliver? Then she glanced at the sheriff of Buck County. Rylan gazed back at her, clear-eyed and determined. She managed a small smile in return. Local law enforcement had done an excellent job so far, and she wasn't going to despair yet.

"Please, I'd like to take Oliver back to Annie's. I'm sure he's hungry."

A baby's fussing carried into the office, underscoring Emily's words.

"No problem. I'll take you over myself." Rylan's gaze turned toward the federal deputies. "Your impostors should be ready to interview by now."

"Don't you want to sit in?"

"I can watch the video later. Or if you want to wait for me, I'll have Steve set you up with a doctor's appointment while you grab a late lunch."

The pair exchanged glances.

"The suspects can marinate for a while," Delgado said. "Lunch sounds great. I hate to go into an interview hungry."

The two deputies grinned at each other, sharing some sort of inside joke that often developed between partners.

"Then we'll check into a local hotel," Carstairs said. "And we'll keep whatever medical appointment your office sets up."

The woman cocked an eyebrow at the other federal deputy, and the man jerked a curt nod.

"Sounds like a plan, then." The sheriff turned toward Emily. "Let's get Oliver home and fed."

A few minutes later, Rylan opened the door for her, and Emily walked into Annie's living room. *Home?* The sheriff had said he was taking them home. This was a nice place and was certainly somebody's home but not hers. When would she figure out where she belonged?

Keeping her thoughts to herself, Emily headed to the guest room and changed Oliver. By that time, the little guy was alternating between sucking furiously on one of his fists and letting out demanding wails.

"Food coming right up, buddy." She carried him into the kitchen.

Her stride hitched as she found Rylan sitting at the table sipping a cup of cold coffee that had been left in the carafe since morning.

"I thought you would have gone back to the office." She situated the fussing baby in a high chair that had been donated by one of the townspeople.

Rylan set his coffee mug on the table. "I wanted to hear from you any insights about the criminal antics this afternoon."

Emily grimaced at him as she fixed cereal for Oliver. "One, I'm extremely thankful Oliver and I never got into that car with those two impostors. And two, I'm going to grab you a pack of frozen vegetables for that bruised cheek."

"I'd forgotten about that," Rylan said as he gingerly touched the slight swelling.

"Well, I haven't, and I never will." She opened the freezer door, grabbed a package and then handed it to him. "You and your people and the entire town keep going above and beyond to protect and serve us—virtual strangers in your midst. Why do you do it?"

She sat down and began feeding Oliver, and his fussing quieted. The sheriff sat, holding the package of frozen peas to his cheek and staring into his coffee while she spooned cereal into the baby's eager mouth. She'd meant her question somewhat rhetorically, but he seemed to be mulling the issue over quite deeply.

Then he lifted his gaze toward hers, and the iron-gray eyes had gone smoky. "The folks around Drover's Creek are hardy stock—independent, tough-minded and loyal to a fault. Oh, we have our internal squabbles and rivalries, but that all goes away when a threat from the outside intrudes. Something about your situation with no memories, no resources and a baby involved has locked their loyalty in on you and Oliver. You're one of *us*, and whatever—*who*ever—is menacing you and Ollie is *them*. It's as simple as that."

"You understand your community well. But what about you? I sense a story, but—well, sorry. I'm prying. Never mind."

Emily fixed her attention on Oliver, who was happily gobbling and drooling bits out the sides of his mouth.

She picked up a napkin and wiped his chin temporarily clean.

"You're right," the sheriff said eventually. "And you're not prying. Up until five years ago, I was a happily married man, but then my wife died, and I didn't—*couldn't*—save her. I can't let that happen again to someone depending on me."

Emily stilled, the spoon halfway to Oliver's open and receptive mouth. The sheriff had gone pale beneath his tan. Whatever had happened was bad and cut deep. Rylan Pierce was a long way from being healed of the wound.

Did he *want* to talk to this woman about the singular most painful event of his life? When was the last time he'd spoken to anyone about the day Sheryl died? How about never?

At the time it happened, he'd responded to condolences from family and friends with a stoic nod and a brief thank-you. Sure, he occasionally reminisced about her life with others who'd been close to them, but discussing the events of the day she passed from this earth didn't happen. He always changed the subject. Why, then, did he have the urge to bare his soul to this woman? Maybe because her pain touched the place in his heart where he stored his own pain.

"I met Sheryl at a state horse auction in Cheyenne a little less than a decade ago." He set the package of peas on the table. "I won't tell you it was love at first sight because it was anything but." A soft chuckle escaped him. "I can still see her face when I outbid her on a quarter horse broodmare of a certain bloodline that we both wanted in the worst way. She had some sharp words for me, and I'm amazed I got out of there without being slapped. All the way home with my new acquisition, I replayed the fire in those blue eyes. Every time I got around that horse, I'd see those eyes. Finally, I couldn't stand it anymore and called the auction house, which had her contact information, and asked someone there to let her know to call me."

"Softy!" Emily chuckled. "How quickly did she get back to you?"

"Two excruciating days later."

"Don't tell me." Emily lifted a hand, palm out. "You sold the horse to her for what she was willing to pay for it."

"Are you kidding me? I won the auction bidding, fair and square." He leaned toward Emily, elbows on the table. "What I did do was ask if she was interested in the mare's first colt."

"Was she?" Emily set aside the empty cereal bowl and began wiping Oliver's face and hands.

"Grudgingly at first, but she became enthusiastic when a foal was on the way. She lived on her folks' horse ranch only about sixty miles from my spread in a county next door to Buck. Pretty soon she was a regular visitor to check on the mare's progress. The mutual attraction started to overshadow the business relationship, and the rest, as the saying goes, is history. The wedding took place the day after the foal was born, and ownership of mare and colt became a moot issue."

Emily lifted the baby from the high chair and sat him on her lap. "How long were you married?"

"A few days past three years. That's how long it took

for us to save up to have a proper honeymoon." He grimaced into his empty coffee cup. "She wanted to go to Hawaii, so that's what we did. Worst decision of my life."

"Were you sheriff then?"

Rylan shook his head. "Deputy and small-time horse rancher."

"I take it something tragic happened on the long-awaited honeymoon."

"You could say that." A shudder rippled through him. "Sheryl was allergic to bee stings and carried an EpiPen everywhere with her. We had it with us on our hike through a forest to visit an extinct volcano. She was trotting along the trail, enthralled by the sights and chattering away like she did when she was happy. Sometimes she scurried ahead of me, and sometimes she lagged behind. But that was typical of our relationship. I was the steady plodder, she was the flitting dynamo. I remember her laughter—" The words snagged in his throat.

A soft touch encased his wrist. Rylan looked down at the dainty hand on his arm, not at all similar to Sheryl's calloused, farm-girl sturdiness yet motivated by the same type of kind heart behind the gesture.

"It's okay. You don't have to tell me."

"Yes, I do." He lifted his gaze to meet hers. The tender compassion radiating from her blanketed him in warmth. "One thing you've probably figured out about me is I finish what I start."

"All right, then," she said. "Let's move into the living room and settle Oliver on his play mat."

"Good idea." The slight delay would give him an opportunity to gain control of his emotions.

A few minutes later, Emily sat on one edge of the sofa, her hands folded in her lap, attentive gaze fixed on him. Rylan settled back into an easy chair across from her.

"The short of it is, she was looking over her shoulder at me when she tripped over a tree root, fell and tumbled down a short incline. The fall wasn't dangerous at all. She could have hopped up, brushed herself off, laughed and continued our hike...except she disturbed a hive of bees on the way down."

"Oh, no!" Emily's hand went to her throat.

"Exactly." Rylan nodded. "They swarmed. I grabbed her up and ran. We were soon away from the bees, but Sheryl was already laboring to breathe from anaphylaxis. I set her down and administered the epinephrine—but, Emily, we only had one EpiPen, and she'd been stung over half a dozen times. I'd been stung more than that, but I wasn't allergic. The venom was too strong for her. I didn't know what else to do but scoop her up and run for help. By the time I reached any type of civilization, it was too late."

His throat closed around the final words as if his wife's symptoms were suddenly his own, the picture of himself staggering into the park's visitor center with Sheryl limp in his arms vivid in his mind.

Emily eyed him gravely. "I know your head knows you weren't to blame, but I also know your heart holds you responsible. Grief often works that way."

"I suspect you know that truth firsthand."

"I...think so, but—" She massaged the bridge of her nose with two fingers. "A tracheostomy might have worked, but it would have been challenging even for someone like me to perform under primitive conditions with improvised tools."

Rylan's heart leaped. "Even for *you*? Emily, are you a doctor?"

She gaped at him. "I must be. I am. No, I don't know." She wrung her hands. "Could I be? But lack of finger-prints on file in the health-care database say I can't be."

They stared at each other, frozen in place. Rylan's cell phone ringtone shrilled, and they both jerked. He pulled out his phone and growled an answer. He didn't need an interruption when he and Emily teetered on the verge of a revelation.

"Sheriff, we've got a situation over here." Annie's voice came out as if she were panting after a run. "Come quickly."

Something like mouse feet scampered up Rylan's spine. What could possibly have happened to throw his normally unflappable dispatcher into a panic?

TWELVE

Emily's breath caught as the sudden tension in Rylan's posture telegraphed trouble. "What's going on?" she asked when the sheriff lowered the cell phone from his ear.

"That's what I would like to know." His brow furrowed, and he tucked his phone into his pocket. "Annie says I need to get back to the office pronto."

"Shall I come with you?"

Rylan shook his head. "You should be fine here while I go put out whatever's caught fire over at headquarters. Keep all the doors and windows locked. We'll maintain surveillance on the house, but it's highly unlikely anyone will try to gain entry in broad daylight—especially since they probably have no idea where we've stashed you and Oliver."

Emily nodded. "Go on then. It'll soon be time for Ollie's afternoon nap, and I think I'll grab one, too."

Rylan strode toward the front door, then stopped with his hand on the knob. "How is your head, by the way?"

"Better every day." She smiled.

The healing, at least, was going well, even if they hadn't gained much ground in stopping the attacks on her and Oliver. The information from the marshals service put a name to their adversary and explained the vast resources arrayed against them, but didn't tell them why the attacks were happening or how to apprehend the escaped-convict weapons dealer. The man remained in the shadows, calling the shots.

The sheriff went out the door, and Emily's hands balled into fists. How she hated this hiding. Yesterday, she'd done something proactive in acting as bait, but they hadn't caught much. Maybe she should be even bolder in drawing the enemy out. Yet that tactic seemed effective at flushing out the minions, not the master. Besides, stronger exposure might put Oliver in danger, and that she could never do.

With a long sigh, Emily settled onto the floor to play with her baby. His dimply grins and excitement in interacting with his mother soon drove Emily's bad mood far away. When the chortles and hand claps started turning into whines and eye-rubbing, naptime had arrived.

Emily scooped him up and took him into the guest bedroom she shared with her son. The room contained a queen-size bed covered in a hand-stitched quilt—courtesy of Annie's church quilting group—a tall dresser, a rocking chair and the donated equipment for the baby, which included a changing table and a small crib with teddy bear bedding. Emily changed Ollie's diaper, then took him out to the kitchen to make him a bottle and finally carried him back to the bedroom.

Settling into the rocking chair, she popped the bottle's nipple into the baby's waiting mouth. In minutes, the suckling slowed down, and Oliver's eyelids closed. Emily jiggled him a couple of different times to urge him to drink more of his bottle before entering dreamland for good. Finally, she let him sleep and took the bottle away. She gently shifted him onto her shoulder and began patting and rubbing his back. The burping process never seemed to wake him when he was determined to sleep. She could be thankful that he tended to sleep well all night, too. Her sweet little boy took care of his mommy that way.

Soon she transferred him into his crib. Then she stretched out on her bed atop the quilt, and sleep softly claimed her.

Emily jerked awake suddenly, her body tense. She'd heard something that wasn't within the parameters of a usual house noise. Willing herself not to stir, Emily strained her ears to pick up any hint of movement. No sound but the ticking of the grandfather clock in the hallway reached her ears.

Her skin crawled in a stillness that seemed unnatural, because she had no doubt something tangible had awakened her. If it was Annie arriving home or Rylan or someone else from law enforcement coming to check on her, stealth would not be a factor. Whoever was here didn't want his presence known until he was ready to pounce. Which could happen at any moment.

Rylan sat behind his desk, one hand scrubbing his chin and the other gripping a pen fit to break it. Big Dave sat in the guest chair across from him, arms crossed over his barrel chest.

"Who would have ever guessed something like this

could happen in our nice, quiet jail?" the police chief rumbled, shaking his head.

"It's not unheard of for a suspect to try to commit suicide after capture. We can be thankful Leota didn't succeed."

Dave snorted. "Came within a few drops of finishing herself off. Now we've got two suspects in the hospital."

"Doc says they'll both recover. I'm more interested in finding out how Leota got the razor-sharp piece of plastic she used on her wrists. It didn't come from inside this building, and she was wearing one of our jail jumpsuits without access to any of her clothes or other belongings."

"If I didn't know better, I'd say maybe Frick or Frack, one of our other guests, slipped it to her," the chief said. "All the prisoners are in adjoining cells. It wouldn't be hard to pass things along. But where would the fake deputies come by such a tool? They were searched and disarmed."

Rylan shook his head with a grimace. "The fake deputies are still in street clothes. We're not about to issue county jumpsuits to them when the feds are going to haul them off. One of them might have had the item hidden inside a suit-jacket seam or something like that. If the object had been inside a pocket, we would have discovered it. We'll have to update our search protocols to cover checking the suspect's clothing for clandestine items like that. When the real deputies get back from eating and checking into a hotel, we'll conduct the interview with the fakes and ask them about the problem."

Dave's thick eyebrows climbed up his forehead. "So you're saying it is possible Frick or Frack could have

been carrying a concealed means of harming themselves or others?"

"Or to facilitate someone else harming themselves.
I figure they gave the item to Leota, pushed a few verbal triggers for her addict's despair and let matters run
their course."

"But why? Leota had already spilled her guts of what
little she knew."

"I don't know." Rylan scowled. "We don't seem to
know the *why* of any of this. Except—" a thought sucker
punched him in the stomach "—the emergency distracted us. It even rushed me away from Oliver and
Emily. What if I'm wrong about the enemy not knowing
her location?" He surged to his feet. "Come on. We've
got to get back to Annie's house."

"Sheriff!" Steve's voice rang out from the squad
room. "My computer is sounding the intruder alarm
at Annie's place."

Rylan charged out the door with the police chief on
his heels, praying they weren't already too late.

Struggling to control her breathing, Emily pressed
her back against the wall next to the bedroom door.
She'd arisen from the bed to creep closer to the door
in order to discern an intruder's approach better. More
soft sounds, including stealthy footfalls coming from
within the house, had confirmed for her that someone
was here who shouldn't be. They were searching for
her and Ollie, and eventually, they would arrive at this
room. She could've kicked herself for leaving the cell
phone Rylan had given her on the coffee table in the living room, but hopefully, the intruder alarm had sounded

at the law enforcement headquarters. But whether help came or not, no option remained but to defend herself and her baby by whatever means necessary.

If someone wanted to get to Oliver, they would have to go through her…and her trusty lamp. The metal bedside lamp was the only item she'd seen in the room that had any potential as a weapon, and she'd snatched it up. At least using the sturdy appliance like a bat was marginally better than throwing a mug of water at an intruder. So as long seconds ticked past, she stood, holding the lamp ready to strike.

A floorboard creaked mere feet from her position. Emily's throat constricted, and her pulse began to rush like a river in her ears. The doorknob started to turn. She lifted her weapon higher.

A squeak came from the crib, and Emily jerked, then forced herself back to stillness. It was only one of those odd noises babies made in their sleep. Oliver was fine, and she meant to ensure he stayed that way.

The intruder must have heard the noise, as the doorknob stopped turning. Silence fell again.

Blackness edged Emily's vision, and she consciously forced herself to take in a full breath and let it out slowly. Her pulse rate dropped, her muscles loosened and her senses cleared.

The doorknob finished turning, and the door swung silently ajar. Thick fingers closed around the edge of the door, pressing it open farther. Then a tall, paunchy figure with long hair caught back in a ponytail and a bushy beard flowing down the front of his leather motorcycle vest stepped into the room, head on a swivel.

Without hesitation, Emily struck. The intruder yelled

out and thrust up an arm to deflect the blow, but he wasn't fast enough. The metal pole crashed into his burly shoulder, staggering him.

But recovery happened quickly. As Emily drew back for a second strike, the man let out a guttural growl, bared yellowed teeth and charged her. His thick body slammed into hers and drove her to the floor.

Emily landed on her back, the breath gushing from her lungs. Her attacker pinned her in place with his knees on her arms, rendering the lamp useless as a weapon. The man's bloodshot eyes bored into hers. A pungent, smoky odor wafted from him, as if he spent large amounts of time in a dive bar somewhere. His sausage fingers closed around her throat, cutting off all oxygen, as Oliver came awake with a wail.

Rylan didn't knock. He thrust the key Annie had given him into the lock and flung the door open. Oliver's cries carried to him from a back bedroom, along with thumps that could be associated with a struggle.

Not bothering to check if Big Dave was still on his heels, Rylan charged up the hallway as he pulled his weapon. The guest bedroom door stood wide open. At a glance he took in the situation. Emily kicked her legs on the floor and bucked for her life against a local low-life, a far-larger assailant, who was choking her out.

Rylan flipped the gun in his hand so he held the muzzle. Then he slammed the butt against the crown of the man's head. The attacker cried out but failed to release his victim. Rylan hit him again, and the man slumped and rolled onto his side on the floor, groaning and gripping his head with both hands. He didn't get to maintain the defensive posture for more than a second when Big Dave lumbered in, grabbed the guy, wrenched his arms behind his back and slapped on the cuffs.

Ignoring the activity between the chief of police and the attacker, Rylan knelt beside Emily. Red marks circled her throat, and air passed in and out of her lungs in wheezes. With eyes wide enough to show the whites all around, she lunged into a sitting position and threw her arms around him. Rylan wrapped her close.

"We got him," he murmured into her soft, herbal-scented hair. "You're all right now."

"I'm not! It's not!" The cries were wrenched from her in hoarse gasps. "This has to stop. I can't do this anymore."

Emily buried her head in his shoulder, and her hot tears wet his shirt. In his crib, Oliver fussed softly in protest over his interrupted nap.

Rylan glared toward the burly man in handcuffs. "Arlen Grange, you may be a burr in the shoe of this community, but I never pegged you as a murdering kidnapper."

Grange bared his teeth. "Yeah, well, a guy'll do a lot for a fifty-thousand-dollar payday."

The words struck Rylan in the solar plexus. Was this Ward Spencer character's next move, posting a bounty on Emily and Oliver? It made sense; the weapons dealer had run through significant personal resources already. He'd be looking to reach out to get others to do his dirty work.

"Wait!" Emily lifted her head and stared up at him. "You know this creep who attacked me? And what's this about a payday?"

"Every community has its lowlife element." Rylan jerked his chin toward the man in cuffs. "Here's one of ours, and he seems to have achieved a new low."

Emily rose to her feet and turned toward the local tough guy. "Is it true about the bounty?"

"Lady, I'd still be warming a stool at Bucky's Bar if I didn't have fifty thousand reasons to be here instead."

"And how did you know where to find me and Ollie?"

The rough man shrugged meaty shoulders. "Word is the guy offering the bounty has tiny surveillance drones zipping all over this community, watching for your location. As soon as a biker scuttlebutt said that you were staying in this house, I didn't waste a second. Too many other guys are hot to collect, and I wasn't about to be beaten to the payday."

Emily stepped closer to Grange, her eyes shooting fire. "And once you'd killed me and grabbed Oliver, what were you supposed to do with him? I can't see you as a babysitter." Her contemptuous gaze raked him up and down. The would-be assassin took a step backward.

Rylan suppressed a smile as he stood beside her. Another one of this woman's surprising talents—skilled and intimidating interrogator.

Grange's gaze fell to his toes. "Well, I—uh—have a number to call."

"A number?" Rylan pounced on the information. "What is it?"

"It's in my vest pocket."

Big Dave, who still had a hand gripping the suspect's elbow, reached toward the greasy vest and gingerly retrieved a folded bar napkin.

He unfolded it and looked at the paper. "Yep, a phone number. No doubt a burner phone or maybe a VoIP number, but the marshals service has the resources to thoroughly check it out. Those federal deputies should be back at headquarters by now."

Rylan frowned. Voice over Internet Protocol communication wasn't traceable, particularly if routed through a VPN, a virtual private network. He couldn't imagine this sly and deadly weapons dealer providing a number that could locate him. Still, Rylan's office needed to pass the information along to the feds. But that wasn't all that needed to be passed along.

Heart heavy, Rylan turned toward Emily, who had gone to the crib and scooped up the baby. "You and Oliver need to accept the protection of the marshals service." She opened her mouth as if to protest, but he held up a forestalling hand. "Now that Ward Spencer has reached into *my* community to recruit his minions, remaining in Drover's Creek is no longer a viable option. I'm sorry."

He put his heart and soul into the final two words.

Emily locked gazes with him, her countenance drawn and bleak. "Does that mean I'll never see you again?"

Rylan swallowed against a tight throat. "Depending on how matters go with this case, that's a very real possibility. For your own good."

"Being here among people who care about Ollie and me was the only good thing in my life. Now, even that is being ripped away." Fresh tears swam in her eyes.

Rylan turned away stiffly before he could yield to the wild impulse to grab Emily and her baby, bundle them into his truck and whisk them far away from danger. At this moment, life on the run *with* them sounded vastly more appealing than life at home *without* them.

THIRTEEN

Emily sat quietly in the passenger seat of Rylan's pickup truck. Driving his duty vehicle with the sheriff's logo on it didn't fit with their attempt to make their travel low-key. The sunrays of a brand-new day bathed Emily's face in a warmth she barely felt. The magnificent pinky golds of the recent sunrise had not moved her at all as the truck followed the federal deputies' unmarked vehicle toward Cheyenne. Emotion, including fear, seemed drained from her. Numbness gripped her from top to toe. Yesterday's attack at Annie's had sent her fragile existence careening in an unwelcome direction.

The arrangements had been made last night, basically without her input, between the US Marshals Service and the law enforcement community of Buck County. The deputy marshals had no room in their vehicle for Emily and Oliver. Their back seat was occupied by the fake deputies on their way to serious consequences for assaulting federal officials and attempted kidnapping. Rylan had volunteered to transport her and Ollie. Besides, they'd reasoned, another armed member of law enforcement in a small convoy could only act as a deterrent against bad guys with big ideas.

The continued presence of the sheriff at her side was the brightest spot in the very dark picture of Emily's life right now. Then again, spending more time with this man she'd come to care for in a way incompatible with her precarious circumstances could be considered a particularly malicious form of torture.

The sheriff's gaze moved regularly between the rearview mirrors as they drove along at a steady pace. Emily shifted in her seat and glanced over her shoulder toward the road behind them.

"No one's back there."

"And that's a good thing. We haven't been followed from Drover's Creek. Would you like to listen to music?"

Emily glanced toward his sober profile. Did he feel the same gloom over their impending separation as she did? Why would he? His county would be a safer, quieter place without her and her problems.

"Music is fine, if you like, but I'm okay without it, too."

"What do you like to listen to?"

A wry laugh left her throat. "I have no idea."

"My bad. Dumb question." He chuckled. "Tell you what. I'll pull up one of my playlists. It's a mix of soft rock, classic country and contemporary Christian music. You can see if anything catches your fancy."

"Sounds good. Thank you."

The knot in the pit of Emily's stomach loosened the slightest bit. Rylan's courtesy and caring always made her feel safe and accepted in a situation that offered nothing but uncertainty. Besides, the eclectic mix sounded appealing. Soon, Emily found herself tapping her feet to the music and once or twice chiming in on the lyrics.

She grinned at Rylan. "I guess I must know some of these tunes."

"And you've got a nice singing voice."

Emily's face heated, and she glanced over her shoulder to check on Oliver in his car seat. The little guy was kicking his feet and waving a rattle in a near-enough keeping of time with the music.

"Ollie's got rhythm," she told Rylan. "And he clearly agrees with me in approving your musical taste."

"Glad to hear it."

They grinned at each other, and Emily's heart did a backflip. What would it be like to enjoy camaraderie every day with this man? She ruthlessly squashed the speculation. Her mind had no business going in that direction.

Soon their mini caravan came to the interstate and entered moderate traffic flow. This early in the morning, their fellow travelers were mostly long-distance truckers, rendering even Rylan's sturdy pickup puny in comparison. The miles churned past beneath their tires. Midmorning came, and Oliver began to fuss.

"Could you let the guys ahead of us know we need to stop to feed and change the baby?" she asked Rylan.

Via hands-free communication, he got on the phone with Deputy Carstairs.

As soon as he hung up, he glanced toward Emily. "There's a truck-stop service island coming up shortly. We can stop there, and you can tend to Oliver while the rest of us top up the gas tanks and pick up beverages and snacks. Anything in particular you'd like?"

"Coffee, for sure. Cream but no sugar."

"You got it."

"But just like with the music, I'm not sure what snacks I like… Wait a minute… An image of dark chocolate passed through my mind's eye. So some type of candy bar along that line. Maybe with nuts in it?"

"I think that could be managed."

The truckers' service island came into view, perched on a knoll between the twin flows of multiple lanes of traffic. Ahead, the deputies' sedan began to flash its turn signal. With a flick of his hand, Rylan did the same, then turned off the music. Only road noise and Oliver's steady whimpering remained. The vehicles began to slow for the exit, and Rylan's shoulders noticeably stiffened, his head turning slightly as he repetitiously scanned all the rearview mirrors.

Emily's tension ratcheted up. "Are we being followed?"

"Unlikely, but one midsize SUV behind us is also turning off. We'll watch and see who is inside when we stop. Looks more like an average family vehicle than a thug-mobile, so probably no threat."

As they entered the vast parking lot, Emily counted multiple buildings. The sprawling complex featured a gas station, a convenience store, a fast-food franchise, a car-and-truck wash and a huge garage with repair bays.

"This is a full-service waystation," she said. "It's like a small town in itself."

"In Wyoming, towns are few and far between. These service islands in the middle of nowhere are necessary for commerce. They'll even have facilities for showering and good, private bathrooms. You should have no trouble finding a clean and convenient place to care for Oliver's needs."

"It will be nice to stretch my legs, too."

Their little caravan drove past the line of diesel pumps for semitrucks and came to a set of gasoline dispensers for regular vehicles. The deputies' sedan pulled up to one, and Rylan glided into the next slot over.

"Wait here." His words halted Emily, and her fingers went still on the door handle. "I need to touch base with the deputies on logistics. One of us needs to fill the tanks and then grab the refreshments while someone guards the prisoners. And one of us should escort you to the bathroom."

"Agreed, but while you're doing that, I'd like to get Ollie out of his seat and grab his bag."

He nodded. "Fair enough. Stick by the truck."

"Yes, Mother Hen."

Hopefully, she'd kept the irritation out of her tone at the reminder. He'd already made his point. What did the sheriff think she was going to do, flit off with Ollie across the open parking lot alone? Then again, he was just doing his job, and she couldn't be more grateful for how well he did it.

Chill out. Don't take your nerves out on the guy with your best interests at heart.

The summer-morning heat embracing her, she walked around the nose of the truck to the rear driver's side. She opened the door, undid the buckles on Oliver's car seat and received the teary-eyed baby into her arms. He sniffled and rubbed his face on her shoulder. Emily cooed comforting words to him and grabbed his bag.

"Cute kid," an unfamiliar masculine voice said behind her.

Gasping, Emily whirled. The medium-sized SUV that had followed them into the truckers' plaza had parked in the next-door bay. A slightly pudgy, balding man stood beside it, pumping gas, his gaze innocent and friendly.

"Thanks," she managed to say with a nod.

Rylan and the deputies stood in front of his truck, and Rylan's gaze periodically slid toward her. His watchfulness was anything but irritating at this moment. Emily hurried in his direction, sparing a glance into the neighboring SUV. A woman sat in the front passenger seat, paging through a magazine. In the back seat, a teenage girl thumbed away at her cell phone's screen. An almost-cliché ordinary family. Emily's insides relaxed.

"Carstairs is going to accompany you," Rylan said. "She'll scope out the situation before you enter the restroom, and she can even go inside with you if need be."

"Makes sense." Emily tamped down her disappointment at separating from the person she trusted above anyone else on the planet and nodded toward the federal deputy. "Lead on."

The woman shook her head with a slight smile. "You go first. I need to keep you in sight at all times as I watch the area around us."

Emily headed toward the convenience store, where the restrooms were likely to be located. The soft tread of the deputy came behind. Stepping into the store, air-conditioning welcomed her, and a prominent sign pointed toward the facilities they were looking for. The place was busy, and she had to dodge around several customers as she made her way toward the back of the building. No one appeared to afford them a second glance. The apparent anonymity was refreshing and comforting.

A hallway turned at a right angle, and Emily followed it. Ahead, the hallway took another sharp turn with an arrow labeled *Showers*. She stopped short of the shower hallway beside a door marked *Women*.

Deputy Carstairs caught up to her and tried the handle. It turned.

"I'll clear the interior," she said and went inside.

Emily waited, bouncing Oliver in her arms. The inspection took only a few seconds. Carstairs reappeared and held the door to permit them entrance.

"There's one window to the outside," the deputy said, "but it's set high and not big enough to offer admittance to any unwanted company. I'll be right here."

Emily carried her baby inside. The room was spartan but clean and offered a wall-mounted changing table. Quickly and efficiently, Emily got Oliver into a clean diaper and then mixed his bottle with purified water from her bag.

"I know you'd like cereal at this time of day," she told Oliver. "But this will have to do for now. Let's go back to the truck, and I'll feed you there while the others finish what they're doing."

Emily unlocked the door and began to draw it open just as a loud grunt came from someone in the hallway. Another someone rammed into the door hard from the other side. Emily staggered backward, squeezing Oliver tight.

The skinny teenager from the SUV barged in and closed the door on noises indicating an ongoing battle in the hallway. But the woman who faced Emily was no teen. Up close, small lines edging hard eyes and a more mature texture of the skin betrayed a greater age than tender teens by at least a decade. Instead of a cell phone, the deceptively young-looking but definitely adult woman gripped a small handgun pointed in Emily's direction.

"Not a word," the woman rasped in a smoker's growl. "You're coming with me."

Emily's pulse skyrocketed, and her vision narrowed on the woman with the gun—not in fear but in fury. What was it with these people wielding guns around a baby?

Time slowed to a crawl.

In an eternal split second, Emily whirled to place her own body between the weapon and the infant as she whipped the heavily packed diaper bag toward the hand that gripped the offending firearm.

Rylan pulled his pickup out of the pump bay and into a parking spot near the entrance to the convenience store. He shut the engine off, opened his door and began to step out, but the blast of a gunshot from inside the building froze him, his foot not quite on the ground. Then electricity rushed through him, and he bounded from the vehicle, leaving the door agape.

He charged for the entrance as screaming customers flooded outside, some through the door he was trying to enter and some from another door farther down. A second shot sounded, sending Rylan's heart into his throat. Drawing his weapon, he fought his way upstream against the stampeding people.

Just over the threshold, he stopped and scanned the area. A few patrons remained inside, crouched behind racks of goods, wide-eyed and frozen in place. The gunshots had come from deeper inside the store. He found the sign for the restrooms—where the weapons had been fired, where Emily and Oliver had gone. Scuffling noises and grunting came from somewhere behind a wall in that location.

Rylan fought the instinct to charge, roaring his anguish like a berserker of old. His training kicked in. Moving with controlled speed and precision, he forged ahead, clearing each space with his head and gun on a swivel as he went. At last, he reached the hidden hallway. The distinctive smack of flesh on flesh, followed by a pained feminine squeal, drew him around the corner, weapon extended.

Carstairs struggled with not one but two female assailants, one thin and petite and the other tall and rawboned. A handgun lay on the floor halfway between his feet and the combatants. The federal deputy landed a kick on the elfin one's solar plexus, driving her backward, gasping for air, as the bigger woman snarled and closed her hands around Carstairs's throat.

"Freeze!" Rylan bellowed, and the chaotic scene suddenly went still.

The federal deputy met Rylan's gaze, and then she calmly broke the other woman's grip around her throat, whirled the suspect around and applied restraints. The other suspect had finally caught her breath and sat slumped against the wall, a surly expression on her face. Carstairs quickly restrained her, as well

"Where are Emily and Oliver?" Rylan asked.

"In the ladies' room," the deputy answered a bit hoarsely.

Pent-up breath escaped Rylan's taut throat. He moved to the closed door and knocked. "Emily?"

No answer. His chest tightened.

"Emily, are you in there? Everything's under control now. You can come out."

Again, no answer.

Rylan tried the doorknob, and it turned. Slowly, he pressed the door open to expose an empty room. He stepped inside and checked behind the door. No one. A glint of something caught his eye from the toilet bowl. He looked down into the water. How had a micro 9mm handgun wound up in the commode? More vitally, where were Emily and Oliver?

"There's no one in here," he called out to Carstairs.

"That's not possible." She appeared in the doorway. Her mouth fell open as her gaze dissected the small room. "She and the baby *were* in here up until I was attacked by one woman while the other went after Emily. My attacker drew a gun. We struggled for the weapon, and it discharged more than once. I disarmed the woman just as the other one came staggering out of the bathroom, and we all engaged each other. Then you showed up. Thank you, by the way."

Rylan nodded in acknowledgment. "Did you have sight of the ladies' room door throughout your altercation?"

Carstairs pursed her lips in thought, then shook her head. "I can't guarantee I did."

"So someone could have taken Emily and the baby, and you might not have seen it happen."

The deputy gave a curt nod.

"Where's Deputy Delgado?" Rylan's gaze searched the area.

"I'm here, Sheriff." The man stepped into the hallway, his gun drawn but held by his side.

"Where have you been?" his partner demanded.

"Defending our prisoners against a touristy-looking guy who brandished a gun like he intended to kill them rather than rescue them. I disarmed him. No shots fired. And he has now joined the party in the back seat of our vehicle. By the glares the trio is exchanging, if they weren't all restrained, they'd likely be going at each other. What's the situation here?"

"Multiple assailants subdued," Carstairs answered.

"Our two charges are missing," Rylan all but bellowed.

Delgado paled. "What… Where… How?" He gazed around as if looking would make them appear.

"We'll have to get the highway patrol involved ASAP." Carstairs swiped a radio from the utility belt under her suit jacket.

"I'm sure they've already been called by some frightened patron or attendant," Rylan said over his shoulder as he hustled out of the hallway and into the store.

No sign of Emily and Oliver. The few people who remained in the merchandise area, including a clerk behind the counter, gazed at him with jittery eyes.

"The danger is over," Rylan told them. "Have any of you seen a woman and an infant pass through here?"

Every head moved back and forth in the negative.

Rylan stepped out into the parking lot, where some people stood in nervous clumps while others headed for their vehicles.

"Remain where you are," he commanded but didn't pause to ensure he was obeyed.

In a slow 360-degree turn, he scanned the area. His gut churned. He couldn't lose Emily and Oliver now. Not only because he was an officer of the law charged with their safety, but also because they meant the world to him. How had that level of personal engagement happened so quickly?

A state-patrol vehicle roared up the entrance way, lights flashing but no siren. A second one pulled in and blocked the exit. The cavalry had arrived but quite likely too late. Whoever had Emily and the baby could well be long gone down the interstate, and no one had any idea what sort of vehicle they might have taken. So much for the possibility of an APB to stop a certain type of transportation. Then again, maybe someone here had seen something. Time to start the interviews of both suspects and bystanders, as well as initiate a thorough search of every inch of the truck plaza.

Rylan holstered the gun he still gripped in his right hand. The splinted injury on his left hand throbbed with the pulsing thunder of the blood in his veins. *Emily, Oliver, wherever you are, I'm going to find you.*

A full hour of furious activity from an ever-increasing number of law enforcement personnel yielded no results. Emily and the baby had effectively vanished.

Insides hollow as an empty gourd, Rylan gazed after the state-patrol vehicle leaving the plaza with the new suspects secured in the back. Then he turned away and trudged to his pickup. He hauled himself inside, then sat, gripping the steering wheel and staring vacantly at the crime scene tape newly crossed over the front doors of the convenience store.

Rylan bowed his head. "God, please protect Emily and Oliver, wherever they are." His voice emerged in a hoarse murmur. "Emily is clever and quick. Offer her a means of escape. Or, if not that, please guide me—us—any of the searchers to them before it's too late. I'm truly desperate, Lord. I—"

"Psst!"

The soft, sharp sound arrested the words in Rylan's throat.

"Psst!"

The insistent noise came from behind him.

"Don't turn around," the voice admonished. "We're on the floor, underneath the throw blanket you keep back here."

Emily! Rylan's heart leaped.

"What are you doing?" he asked. "We've been hunting everywhere for you. I thought you'd been taken."

"I know. I'm sorry," Emily whispered. "It's best if everyone thinks we've disappeared. That way the bad guys won't have a clue where we are. Don't let anyone here know we're all right. Don't call the marshals service. Don't even call your people in Buck County. Just get us out of here and take us somewhere safe."

"Roger that."

A grin formed on Rylan's face. Emily and the baby

were okay, and they were right here with him. Then the grin faded. Someone in law enforcement was colluding with the enemy, or the bad guys wouldn't have known Emily and Oliver were being transported to Cheyenne or found them at this truck plaza.

"Start the pickup and let's go so Ollie and I can get out from under this blanket and into the air-conditioning." Emily's tone had gone snippy. "It's roasting hot back here. If Oliver weren't sound asleep, he'd be bawling up a storm."

Rylan stifled the returning grin and started the engine. A rap sounded on his window, and he rolled it down to speak with a taut-faced Delgado.

"We'll be taking the deputy-impersonators on to custody in Cheyenne," the man said. "An alert has gone out statewide for the subjects."

"Emily and Oliver."

"Right."

"I'll head for home," Rylan said. "There's nothing further I can do here."

"Agreed." The deputy nodded. "And…I'm sorry things worked out this way."

"Me too."

Rylan powered up his window and pulled away. Soon they were back on the interstate, now heading in the opposite direction.

"You should be able to come out from under the blanket now and get Oliver strapped into his car seat."

"I'll take you up on that offer."

A moment later, Emily's sweat-soaked face appeared in his rearview mirror. Clicks and some mild baby whimpers signaled her securing the sleeping child.

"Tell me what happened," Rylan said.

Another click answered him—Emily securing herself.

"Does it ever feel good to breathe cool air," she said with a soft moan. "Okay, here's the story. The SUV that followed us into the truck plaza contained a middle-aged man, a big woman and a petite female passing herself off as a teenager. As I was coming out of the bathroom, the fake-teenager lady barged in, pointing a dinky gun. Of course, when the business end of a firearm is staring at you, it looks bigger than it is."

Rylan furrowed his brow. "How did the gun get into the toilet bowl?"

"I chucked it there after I knocked her for a loop with the diaper bag, and she dropped it."

He spurted out a laugh. Could he believe his ears? Then again, with Emily, the unexpected was to be expected—like clocking a behemoth with a mug of water from a hospital bed. "You did what?"

Emily sniffed. "I wasn't about to let some creeper wave a gun around in the presence of a baby. Once I knocked her down, I tossed the weapon into the nearest repository where it was least likely she'd care to retrieve it."

Unless he missed his guess, Emily's tone sounded the slightest bit cocky. Not without good cause, however.

"And then what?"

"I left the bathroom to find Deputy Carstairs battling the bigger woman for control of a gun. The weapon went off, assassinating a ceiling tile, and the whole place went berserk. I slotted Oliver and me into the scramble to escape. I glimpsed you trying to get inside through one entrance while I was going out another. Your pickup was sitting in a parking spot with the door ajar—not a good idea, by the way, but handy for me—so I leaped inside and hid under the blanket in the back seat. While everyone around was throwing a conniption fit, I sat there and fed Oliver his bottle. Then he fell asleep, and I waited until you finally got into your truck."

"And here we are," Rylan said, "basically on the run from everybody."

"True, but there is one enormous gain in all the mess."

"What's that?"

"I've remembered." Emily's tone went thin and strained. A ragged sniffle followed the words.

Rylan went rigid. "You remembered what?"

"Everything."

FOURTEEN

"A part of me wishes I were still a blank slate."

Emily closed her eyes and concentrated on breathing. The simple act of being alive was almost more than she could bear when those she loved had gone and left her all alone. Yes, she *had* been married to a military man, and the notice of his sacrificial death *had* thrown her into catastrophic labor. Her dream was all too tragically true.

As she had fled from the gunfire in the truck plaza— bearing an infant who depended on her—and taken shelter in Rylan's vehicle, the memories had flooded over her like a tsunami, nearly drowning her in pain and sorrow. After her time of perfect forgetting, the sudden remembering refreshed every ounce of grief as if she were experiencing it for the first time.

"Emily!" Rylan's voice prompted, and she opened her eyes.

"It's Erin. Erin McGrath. Dr. Erin McGrath."

"Hello, Erin. I'm pleased to meet you."

"'Pleased'? After all the trouble I've brought with me?"

"Definitely pleased…and honored to be of service."

Warmth lapped against the cold emptiness in her core. "Thank you."

"You *are* a doctor, then."

"A pathologist, to be precise."

"Then why were your fingerprints not in the system?"

"I'm from Halifax, Nova Scotia."

Rylan snorted. "As simple as that."

"No. Nothing about my situation is simple or easy."

"As our experiences these past few days have proven." He paused, and she caught his gaze seeking to meet hers in the rearview mirror. "Then I suppose you know—"

"Who Oliver's mother is? No, I don't."

Rylan's brow furrowed; then he let out a long sigh. "Not you, then."

"Not me-e." Her voice cracked with the confession. Another grief to pile on top of the rest.

"I'm so sorry." His tone wept sincerity.

Erin reached out and folded her fingers around the baby's tiny hand. "It's him I feel sorry for. I assume it was his mama those thugs killed before I snatched him away from them. We don't even know his real name."

"Oliver will do for now."

"Yes, it will. That's the name I think of him by— and honestly, even though I know better now, I still feel like his mother."

"Understandable. Now that everything has come back to you, do you remember any details that might help us end the threat to you and Oliver?"

Erin's breath caught. She'd been wallowing so thoroughly in the emotional swamp of her personal losses she hadn't taken the time to consider how useless the return of her memories was to her current situation. The major breakthrough in her mind accomplished nothing toward keeping her and Oliver safe. A ruthless man out there still wanted her dead and to take the baby.

A thousand questions about Erin's backstory buzzed through Rylan's thoughts, but right now, those were distractions. He needed to stay focused on what pertained to protecting her and Oliver.

"What do you remember about the night you witnessed the murder and grabbed Oliver?" He restated his question.

"I'd checked into the Western Lodge in Burling, dog-tired from driving all day on the way to my new job as a medical examiner in Boise, Idaho."

"M. E.!" Rylan burst out. "Is that what the embroidered initials on your scarf stood for?"

Erin let out a soft laugh. "Quick deduction, Sherlock. The embroidered silk scarf was a going-away gift from my colleagues in Halifax. After everything that had happened, they were happy for my opportunity to start over in a new place and to be the chief medical examiner rather than a subordinate."

After everything that had happened? Rylan wasn't going to ask what that meant. Not yet, anyway. He had his suspicions if that dream of hers reflected reality, but he hoped he was wrong. This was not the time to delve into what must be the most tender of subjects for her.

"Sorry for the detour off-topic."

"No problem. You're probably wondering why I was driving cross-country rather than flying into Boise."

"Yes, but—"

"I had a month before I needed to start my new position, so I flew to New York, then decided to rent a car and take a road trip. See the US and clear my head. To accomplish that, my route was meandering, and I took smaller roads, not interstates. And I traveled light. All my things had been trucked ahead in a portable shipping container that would be waiting for me in Boise when I arrived."

Rylan frowned. "Buck County, Wyoming, is south of the route to your destination."

"Not if you're planning to visit your aunt Emily and uncle Joe in Ogden, Utah, first."

"Your aunt's name is Emily? That's probably why the name seemed familiar to you, and you claimed it. Your aunt and uncle would be missing you, then?"

"No. I didn't give them a firm date of my arrival. Just said I'd call them when I got close. But back to the night of the murder. As I said, I had checked into the motel and planned to head straight to bed, but first I wanted a bottle of water from the vending machine outside."

"That's when you witnessed the murder?"

"Not exactly. On my way up the sidewalk, I heard a woman cry out from somewhere in the parking lot around the corner of the building, and I hurried to see if someone was hurt. Just before I turned the corner, there was a strange sound—something between a loud cough and a muted firecracker."

"A gunshot from a suppressed firearm."

"I would assume so."

"You didn't actually see the men shoot the woman?"

"No, I didn't. When I stepped into view of the situation, the woman lay sprawled on the tarmac, unmoving, and a pair of men in dark suits stood over her. I did see a gun in one of their hands."

"Did you see their faces?" Rylan searched Erin's expression through the rearview mirror.

"Just the backs of their heads. They were arguing with each other. One guy said they needed to 'dispose of the body.'" She bracketed the last four words in air quotes. "The other guy said they needed to 'just grab the kid and get out of there.'" Again, the air quotes. "They hadn't seen me yet. I was standing there, frozen in shock, but at the mention of a child, I began looking around and spotted Oliver in his car seat sitting off to the side. Something fierce rose up inside of me."

She began shaking her head. "No way was a couple of murderous thugs going to make off with a baby under my watch. So I snatched him up and ran. *Then* they saw me and took a shot at me. You know the rest. I took that junk car and ended up in the middle of nowhere in your county." She frowned. "Listening to my own story, I can see I won't be much of a witness against anybody as far as legal prosecution."

Rylan grimaced and shook his head. "But they don't know how little you saw."

"I can understand that, but I don't understand *why* they want Oliver."

"We need to find out—but in the meantime, we need to stash you and the baby someplace safe."

"Where would that be?"

"Exactly where I told Annie I was going when I spoke to her on the phone before climbing into my pickup at the truck plaza. My ranch. You can meet my family—Sheba, the Australian shepherd, and Hank and Pearl, my quarter horses."

"Sounds lovely."

"Sounds temporary. You can only hide out with me for so long. Within days, maybe even hours, we need to get new identities for you and Oliver and relocate you. The problem is that I don't know how to accomplish that without involving other people. So far, bringing others into the mix hasn't worked out too well."

Erin's stomach scrunched in on itself, her emotions reeling all over the place. Emily, the blank slate, had found a home in Drover's Creek with people who loved and accepted her even while knowing little about her. Erin, the bereft, had no clue how to fit the Emily episode into her life's narrative. Now she was expected to leave Erin and Emily behind and become someone new in an undetermined location where she would be a stranger. And she would never again be a doctor. Unacceptable.

"No!" The word burst from her lips. "I'm not running, and I'm not hiding. I'm going to reclaim my life. I'd like to be able to do that with Oliver in my custody, but I have no legal claim on him, and I want him to be safe." Tears stung the backs of her eyes at the mental picture of placing the precious child into the arms of someone else. Permanently. "Let's concentrate on finding him a haven." The sentence came out as if her voice had gone a bit rusty.

Wearing a frown, Rylan glanced at her over his shoulder. "How about we get you home to my place and talk it over there?"

"I don't think anything's going to change between here and there."

"You never know."

Silence fell in the vehicle. Soon they left the interstate for a smaller highway. The western Wyoming prairie land punctuated by dry washes and rock heaves flowed past the windows. Sagebrush and cattle dotted the landscape. In the distance, the outskirts of the Rocky Mountains jutted in bluish spikes against the horizon.

Without him saying anything, the twitch along Rylan's jaw communicated his frustration with the situation. No doubt he longed to ask her more questions about herself, but Erin's respect for the man reached new heights when he declined to pry. Maybe later she would tell him more. Right now, she needed to process being herself again, with all the baggage that entailed. And even more, she needed to take stock of the feelings she'd developed for Rylan. Now that she was back to being Erin, how seriously should she take those feelings that had developed when she was Emily? Weren't Emily and Erin the same person—herself? Oddly, they seemed disconnected in her psyche, leaving her disoriented, to say the least.

Oliver woke up with a start and began to fuss. They weren't about to stop for anything until they reached Rylan's ranch, so, thankful for the distraction from thoughts that were giving her a headache, Erin strove to entertain the unhappy infant. At last they rolled up Rylan's meandering driveway toward a long ranch house with a spacious porch that stretched across the whole front of the mist-blue building trimmed with glossy black shutters.

Erin gazed around at the neatly maintained property, with its small, metal-sided machine shed to one side of the house and a hip roofed barn on the other side. A pair of horses—one reddish-brown and the other one dappled gray—loitered, tails swishing, in a corner of a fenced-in pasture attached to the barn. Hank and Pearl, no doubt. As they reached the carport, a medium-sized black-and-white dog with golden markings loped up to the truck, pink tongue lolling around a doggy grin. Sheba.

"Climb on out," Rylan said. "Sheba won't bother you—other than trying to sniff you."

"No problem." Erin opened her door, admitting a mixture of fresh hay and sage smells, along with the dry heat. "I like dogs."

She stepped onto the cement under the carport roof, offered the back of her hand to Sheba and then laughed at the tickle of hot breath and whiskers against her skin. The dog's bushy stub-tail wagged as she pranced with her front paws.

"You are such a pretty girl." Erin scratched between the animal's floppy ears. "One beautiful blue eye and one green like mine."

Oliver's increased crying drew Erin's attention, but Rylan beat her to the rescue as he retrieved the wiggling baby from the truck. Sheba abandoned Erin and trotted around to meet the noisy newcomer. Erin followed the dog. Hopefully, the dog and baby encounter would go all right.

Rylan squatted, cradling Oliver in one arm and controlling his dog with the other. The animal seemed to sense the need for gentleness and stretched forth her nose to just within reach of the baby's pudgy fingers. Ollie extended an arm and batted his palm against the dog's face, his fusses turning to giggles. Erin's insides relaxed.

If only Oliver could grow up in such a wholesome environment surrounded by wide open spaces. Wouldn't it be nice if she could enjoy such a life with him?

Whoa, girl! She had a job and the prospects of a new life waiting for her in Boise. She'd never lived in a rural area. Why would she be yearning for it now?

Then she looked at the smiling man cradling the infant in his arms. Her inner world tilted and then righted itself. Suddenly, Erin merged with Emily in strange new desires for her future and whom she wanted in it. Too bad the dream lay far out of reach.

From a seat at his kitchen table, Rylan gazed at Erin as she prepared to bathe Oliver in the sink. They'd enjoyed simple lunch meat sandwiches together. Now she hummed as she prepared the baby's bathwater while Oliver looked on—kicking and cooing—from his infant seat.

She looked so natural in his house, and she liked the place even though it wasn't much. Just an open-plan living room, dining and kitchen space, with a hallway leading off to a pair of bedrooms, a decent-sized bathroom and a small office. Sheryl had liked it here, too, but she'd often talked of building onto the house after they started having kids. They'd had a designated savings account, scrounging together their nickels and dimes for that very purpose. The account still existed. He'd never been able to bring himself to touch it. Now…

well, now nothing had changed. Emily and Oliver would be leaving soon. They didn't have the option to stay.

Rylan rose, pushing his chair away from the table with the backs of his knees. Em—no, Erin—blinked at him over her shoulder.

He offered her a smile. "I'm going to go outside and check on the horses. I'm sure their stalls need mucking."

She wrinkled her nose at him. "Sounds like fun."

"I find it good exercise and mentally relaxing at the same time. Call me if you need me." He pointed toward the burner phone he'd given her a couple of days ago that now sat near the place at the table she'd occupied while they ate.

"Will do." She turned back to her preparations, and Rylan stepped out the side door from the small mudroom attached to the kitchen.

He walked through the carport and into the dirt yard between the house and the barn. Little puffs of dust sprang up beneath his boots with every step. The area could use a good rain but wasn't likely to get one for a while. Not the season for it. He could be thankful his place had a good, deep well. The skin on the back of his neck prickled with more than just the heat of the sun, and he stopped in the middle of the yard between the house and the barn. His gaze scanned the area, but he didn't see or hear anything out of place. He proceeded on his way, his senses ratcheted up on high alert.

The stall-mucking went smoothly, but the tension never quite left him. However, he did a lot of thinking about the predicament Erin, Oliver and he found themselves in. Decisions had to be made and protective provisions put into place—no way around it.

He hung the pitchfork on the wall and parked the wheelbarrow, then pulled out his phone. First, he called Annie in Dispatch and let her know he had arrived home. She asked if there was any news on Emily and Oliver, and he told her the marshals service and highway patrol were looking. She could kill him later for his omission of other details, like their presence with him, but he no longer trusted their communications system. Somehow, law enforcement on this case was being monitored. No one could know his charges' new location.

Then he made two calls of a different nature—one to a contact he knew who could provide new identification and relocation for Erin and Oliver, if Erin consented to go that route. The other call he made to a close friend with special skills. He made no call to the marshals service, and they wouldn't be happy with him, but he didn't care. Protecting Erin and Oliver came first.

After he disconnected his final call, his phone rang. Erin.

"Hello. Everything okay?"

Her breathing rasped loud and fast in his ear. Rylan's spine stiffened, and the air froze in his lungs.

"Come quickly. I may have discovered why this crook needs to get his hands on Oliver."

FIFTEEN

"It's fading," Erin told Rylan the moment he came through the door.

"What's fading?" Rylan's brow puckered as he came to a halt in the middle of the kitchen, staring at her where she stood near the sink, cradling Oliver in her arms.

"Oliver's belly birthmark." She stepped closer to Rylan with the baby. He was squeaky clean, wearing only a diaper and cooing around a fist in his mouth. "While I was bathing him, I noticed. See?"

Rylan gazed down at the child's tummy. "I'll have to take your word for the fading. This is the first time I've seen the mark. Except..." He leaned closer. "It's like there are darker squiggles mixed into the oval splotch."

"That's the thing. The entire oval used to be nearly black. Now it's going gray with tiny darker streaks mixed in."

"This must be one of those high-end, noninvasive temporary tattoos that last a few weeks."

"I agree with you, but I think the darker marks mean something. We need a magnifying glass."

"I've got one in the office." He strode away and up the hallway.

Erin deposited the baby in his infant seat and strapped him in. He fussed and squirmed against the restraints, but they needed him relatively still for the examination.

"Just a few minutes, sweetie. Then I'll feed you your cereal."

Rylan returned with the magnifying glass and held it out to her.

She waved him toward the baby. "You do the honors. I'm too nervous to hold the glass still. I feel like we're on the verge of a breakthrough."

"You could be right." He flickered a smile at her and leaned over Oliver's plump tummy.

Soon, Rylan began making humming noises, and Erin wrung her hands together.

"Letters, right? Some sort of message?"

"Letters, yes, and quite a few numbers, too."

"Like the message is in code?"

"No, I think it's a bitcoin-wallet address. Thirty-four distinct marks, but I can't quite read them all. I need a stronger magnifying glass, and I think the main portion of the tattoo needs to fade a little more before it will be completely legible."

"A bitcoin-wallet address!" The interior of Erin's mouth soured, and she curled her lip. "So this whole mess is over money. How disgusting."

Rylan straightened up and grinned at her. "I like your attitude, but with a guy like Ward Spencer, everything comes down to money."

She sniffed. "As naive as it sounds, a teensy part of me had hoped someone was after the baby for himself. Because they wanted *him*."

"The money motive doesn't explain why the tattoo

was placed on this specific child. Oliver himself must have significance to Spencer. However, the fading tattoo *does* tell us why the weapons dealer is in such a rush to grab him. He's been burning through resources at a reckless rate, almost to the point of exposing himself to capture. The clock is ticking, and soon the markings will fade away entirely. If he doesn't retrieve the address before it's gone, no one will be able to open the wallet ever."

Erin ground her teeth together and crossed her arms tightly over her chest. "He's going to continue attempting to hunt us down like a rabid animal. I've forgotten what it's like to feel safe."

Rylan's hands settled on her shoulders and squeezed. The firm warmth of the touch loosened the tight knot in her belly.

"I'm working on a plan to hide you out, away from anyone you've ever met."

She scowled at him. "I told you I don't want to leave my life behind and become someone else."

"Discovering the tattoo changes everything. If we can keep you both safe until the mark fades, Spencer will have no more reason to come after Oliver, and I think he'll give up on you, too, and go back into hiding."

Erin gazed up into Rylan's earnest face. Did she dare hope for freedom to pursue her life? And what would that pursuit look like? A prominent but hectic position as a pathologist in a metro area? Or did a change of pace appeal to her as much as the man in front of her did?

Rylan's expression softened, and she yielded as he drew her closer to himself. Slowly, his head lowered toward hers, his gaze seeking permission. She raised up on her tiptoes to meet him.

Then he froze, lips hovering over hers. He tilted his head as if listening for something. She held her breath and heard it too: helicopter rotors. Her heart rate bumped into overdrive, and she stepped away from the sheriff's welcoming arms.

His mouth flattened. "Someone's coming, and it's not the cavalry."

Rylan's stomach roiled. So much for gliding home under the radar with no one aware of their location. While he was walking to the barn, he should have given more weight to that eerie sensation on the back of his neck that someone was watching the ranch. Probably had been for days. Now they were about to get a visit from unwelcome company.

"Lock the kitchen door, then call Annie at the sheriff's department." He waved toward Erin's phone on the table. "I'll round up defensive weaponry."

Rylan strode to his office and quickly opened the massive gun safe in the corner. His duty weapon would serve fine as a handgun, but he needed something long-range. His Accuracy International AT-X, with its ten-round double-stack magazine, would fit the bill. He grabbed it, along with some extra ammunition, and set the items on his desk. Then he donned his protective vest and filled the pockets with the ammo clips. He plucked the smaller vest constructed for a female body from a rack. Then the lightweight Mark V Camilla rifle Sheryl used to use caught his eye, but he rejected it. To his knowledge, Erin had no training with firearms.

But anyone could wield a shotgun. His Mossberg 500 would do well for her. He snatched it and started to turn away, then paused.

What if the enemy gained access to the house and close-quarters combat became necessary? *Please, God, don't let it come to that.* Nevertheless, he strapped his KA-BAR tactical knife to his thigh. Better to be prepared.

The chopper noise grew ever louder and closer. Rylan's insides throbbed with the rhythm of the whirling blades that carried the enemy to his doorstep.

In all the years he'd been in law enforcement in Buck County, he'd never had to gear up like he was back in the military. Today, he was glad of the training. This was not suspect apprehension. This was war.

With a frustrated cry, Erin tossed the cell phone onto the table. There was no reception, and the call wouldn't go through. She'd tried three times.

The helicopter's thunder drew closer. Outside, the dog was barking up a storm. Inside, the baby was howling. Erin put her fingers to her temples and rubbed. Her head ached, fit to burst.

Rylan reappeared in the kitchen, his arms laden with weapons, and he was wearing tactical gear. He placed a shotgun on the table. Erin didn't know much about firearms, but she recognized that one.

"For you. And put this on, too." He handed her a bulky vest. "Did you get ahold of Annie?"

Erin shook her head. "There's no service."

The sheriff let out a low growl. "These people must be using a signal jammer. I'm going out to the pickup to use the radio. In the meantime, put on the vest, then do the rounds and make sure all windows and doors are locked and pull all the curtains and shades."

"Got it." Erin grabbed his arm. "Be careful out there."

"You know I will." He patted her hand and headed for the mudroom.

Erin turned away and brushed a comforting hand down Oliver's pudgy cheek, then donned the awkward vest. Next, she headed for the living room to start checking windows. A sudden blast stopped her in her tracks. Rifleshot.

Rylan! Was he okay?

Another shot rang out, this time accompanied by a tinkling of glass. The truck taking a hit? She whirled for the side door where the sheriff had gone out. *No!* She stopped herself midstride. Her first priority was securing the house. She had to trust Rylan to take care of himself.

Heart flailing against her ribs, Erin rushed to the front door and found it already locked and the dead bolt in place. She headed for the curtain pull for the living room picture window, and a third shot resounded—this one originating beside the house—and its timbre was different from the first two blasts. Rylan returning fire.

Erin closed the drapes, and the room went dim. Then she turned to head deeper into the house to secure windows. As she passed into the kitchen, the sheriff stumbled in the door, dragging Sheba with him.

She hurried over to him. "Are you all right?"

"Fine." He jerked a nod. "But I felt the breeze by my cheek with that first bullet. Someone out there is a decent shot and has a line of sight on the carport. I couldn't get to the radio."

Erin firmed her jaw. "We'll have to hunker down and defend ourselves here. Surely someone will report the shots fired."

"We can hope, but rifle fire isn't that unusual around here. One thing we've got going for us is the reluctance they've shown all along to harm Oliver. I don't think they'll shoot directly into the house."

"I pray you're right. But if all they want is the bitcoin-wallet number, why do they care about not hurting Ollie?"

A muscle jumped in Rylan's jaw. "I don't know. Let's finish securing the house."

Working together, they soon made sure all the windows were locked and covered, shrouding the house in dusk. Their eyes would simply have to adjust to the dimness. They wouldn't be turning on any lights to allow their shadows to show against the curtains or blinds.

Erin rejoined Rylan in the kitchen and began rocking Oliver in his seat. The helicopter's roar sounded straight overhead. The house seemed to shudder with the rotor draft. Then the thunder moved off slightly and began to power down to a whine.

"Tuck the baby between the refrigerator and the wall," Rylan said. "There should be enough room if you move the mop, bucket and broom."

Erin scurried to obey, her sidelong looks following Rylan's shadowy figure as he went to the picture window, tugged a corner of the curtain aside and peered out.

"What do you see?" she asked.

"They set the chopper down out front, blocking the

driveway, but no one has emerged yet." He took a knee and raised the rifle to his shoulder.

A fierce emotion swept through Erin. What was it? Pride? Not in herself, no. But in this man who stared death in the eye and prepared to shoot back to defend others. Exactly the sort of person her husband had been. One of the many reasons she'd loved him but now a major reason she couldn't allow herself to yield to her attraction for Rylan. Experiencing such loss again would destroy her. Then again, maybe it was only this sort of man who attracted her. A catch-22.

"Hello, the house!"

The bellow through some sort of radio or bullhorn jerked Erin's thoughts away from personal fears.

Silence fell, which was disconcerting in this unnatural dimness in the middle of the day. Fingers flexing and releasing, Erin tiptoed up behind Rylan.

"Stay down," he hissed over his shoulder, and she dropped to all fours.

"Give me Noah, and I'll let the woman live," the voice bellowed again.

Noah? Erin looked back toward where the baby was hidden in the kitchen. So that was his given name. Her nostrils flared. Maybe this criminal creepazoid knew Ollie's—no, Noah's—real name, but he didn't know that little precious one like she did, and he sure didn't care about him. The crook had ordered Noah's mother murdered.

Erin marched back to the kitchen table and snatched up the shotgun. Over her dead body would this guy get his hands on the baby she loved like she would have loved her own.

* * *

Rylan held perfectly still, regulating his breathing. The sun's rays glinting off the helicopter's glass prevented him from seeing inside the bird, but at the slightest suggestion of a weapon peeking out, he would take a shot.

"I've got four trained shooters with me and a sniper on the hill," said the voice. "There's no escape, and no one is coming to help you. Give me the baby, and we'll leave. Everyone's happy."

Rylan snorted. "And I'll sell you the Golden Gate Bridge for a buck," he murmured under his breath, his offer as sincere as the one from the man in the helicopter.

Was this guy another lackey of Spencer's or—

"Sheriff Pierce!" The bellow rose to greater decibels. "You have five minutes to bring me my grandson—not a second longer, or we will annihilate you."

Yep, it was the man himself, finally doing his own dirty work. *His grandson?* There was the reason Spencer's minions had been hampered by an order not to hurt the baby. Several puzzle pieces now fit together nicely. Spencer's son had been killed by the ATF, so his girlfriend or wife—whichever—fled with their baby and the key to an untold amount of money in a bitcoin wallet. Now, Grandpa wanted the wallet and his heir, and he was willing to do whatever it took to make that happen.

The man would have to get used to disappointment.

There! Someone very large was creeping out the far side of the helicopter. Judging by his size, it was the man who had attacked him and Erin in the hospital.

Rylan shoved the muzzle of his rifle into the window, shattering a corner of it. Then he sent a shot toward the chopper. Dust kicked up at the feet of the man-mountain, who staggered backward behind the cover of the helicopter's body. Too bad for the dude that Rylan could still see the guy's feet. He took a second shot and missed, but the man spooked and disappeared inside. From the jerk of the big bird, Rylan might have hit a strut on the chopper. Not enough to disable it but enough to strum the nerves of their attackers.

Then chaos broke loose.

Armed figures poured out from the helicopter, firing as they ran. Bullets shattered the front window and slammed into the outside walls. Rylan ducked down. So much for not shooting at the house. Spencer must be trusting that Erin and he would have taken precautions with the baby. He was right. Little Noah would stay snug and safe in the nook by the refrigerator.

Something heavy began ramming into the side door, and Erin's shotgun roared. A masculine voice yelped, and the ramming ceased. Someone from the chopper must have reached the house. Where were the others?

Rylan peered outside to find one of the attackers seeking cover behind the machine shed. Rylan took a shot at him just as glass shattered in a back bedroom. His heart climbed into his throat. He couldn't defend the front and back at the same time, and Erin needed to keep the shotgun trained on the side door.

Then vicious snarling rang through the house, followed by a high-pitched scream. *Way to go, Sheba!* Rylan had never heard that tone from his dog—but then, their place had never been attacked before.

Suddenly, a different type of rifle boomed, and a

man cried out from somewhere on his porch. Rylan's lips spread in a wolfish grin. He knew that gun—a FN SCAR 17S. With that weapon in the hands of his neighbor and good buddy, DeMarcus Dobbs, this shooting match was over. Rylan's own personal cavalry had arrived.

SIXTEEN

Seated at Rylan's kitchen table, Erin quelled another bout of internal shivering as she brought a spoonful of cereal to Oli—er, Noah's eager mouth. She was still getting the effects of her adrenaline dump under control. Of course the little guy had been terrified by all the loud noises, but now that things had calmed down, filling his belly had his entire attention.

The firefight concluded more with a whimper than a bang. DeMarcus, the sheriff's friend and a former military sniper, quickly intimidated Ward Spencer's henchmen with his outstanding marksmanship. Rylan told her he'd subdued the sniper on the hill as well, before taking the man's place, but on the good-guy side of things. With a friendly force as a sniper, the others dropped their guns and put their hands up. Even the oh-so-scary man-mountain didn't care to risk having a body part sniped clean off. Maybe because he was an extra-large target.

When the master crook attempted to escape in the helicopter, Rylan displayed some marksmanship himself and put a bullet in the rotor assembly. With the chopper grounded, he personally cuffed the illegal weapons dealer, who immediately began whining for his lawyer. And Sheba? Well, she'd been discovered standing guard, teeth bared, over a terrified and somewhat-bloodied bad guy cowering in the corner of the guest bedroom. The man Erin had shot through the kitchen door was having pellets removed from his legs at the hospital, but he would live. Incredibly, though several of the thugs required medical treatment, no one had lost their lives in the skirmish.

Erin smiled as she shoveled more cereal into Noah's mouth. *Thank You, Lord.*

The sheriff's people, plus some helpers from the city police, had come and gone with all the suspects, no doubt straining the capacity of the Buck County jail even though some of the thugs were in the hospital. According to Rylan, the overcrowding situation wouldn't last long because federal agents from the DEA, the ATF and the marshals service, as well as a set of federal crime scene techs, were on the way via a pair of helicopters. The alphabet soup of agencies all had some interest in this case to protect. They'd take over processing the scene at the ranch and eventually whisk away most of the crooks, including the grand prize, Ward Spencer. The man would return to prison immediately to finish the sentence he'd been meant to serve prior to his escape, and he would also go back to court to be held to account for his most recent criminal escapades.

Noah's eyelids began to droop as he finished his meal, so Erin wiped his face and rocked his infant seat until he went to sleep. Then she slipped him out of the carrier and took him to the dimness and relative quiet of Rylan's bedroom to continue his nap on a soft blanket on the floor, since no crib was available. Returning to the kitchen, she found Deputy Lawrence making tea. The woman had remained behind to keep Erin company because the sheriff felt the need to ride with the suspects to the lockup, and Erin wouldn't budge from the house until Noah had been fed. Now they'd have to postpone departure from the ranch until the baby awakened. Erin gratefully accepted a mug of tea from Sarah and inhaled a long whiff of the aromatic steam.

With her own mug in hand, the woman took a seat across from her. "It's going to take some time to get used to calling you Erin rather than Emily." Sarah smiled. "I'm glad you're all right and you've remembered who you are, though."

Erin took a sip of the tea, and any residual chill from the recent shocking events melted away. "Me too." Rylan's people had been given an abbreviated version of her actual identity. "Do you need to take a statement from me now?"

The deputy shook her head. "I'm told the marshals service wants the first crack at that."

"I can hardly wait."

Sarah laughed and Erin joined in. How nice to share a moment of humor, with no cloud of danger hanging over her head.

"Do you know what the US district marshal told the sheriff who passed it along to the rest of us in the office?" the deputy asked.

"I'm all ears."

"The marshal's personal assistant wasn't the information leak. She really was ill the day the federal deputies got ambushed. But they did a sweep and discovered a listening device in the woman's office like the one that got planted here in our headquarters."

"So no cops on the take. Glad to hear it."

"Us, too, but the marshals service is plenty embarrassed, and they've upped their monitoring protocols like we have. I don't advise mentioning the incident when you give your statement. They're going to be touchy on the subject."

Erin chuckled. "Gotcha loud and clear."

"So what are you going to do now that the danger is over and you've got your identity back?" Sarah leaned forward, her eyebrows scrunched together as if she were peering into Erin's head for the answer.

Erin frowned into her tea. "That, Sarah, is the large and urgent question I'm going to have to deal with sooner rather than later."

She had a job waiting for her in Idaho, but if she went there without little Noah, the fresh start would be meaningless. And she'd miss Drover's Creek—more specifically, the people she'd met here. One in particular.

An ache began in her heart and spread through her chest. Not a medical condition but an emotional one. Ever since her life in Nova Scotia had shattered, grief dogged her every step, and it had not left or lessened. If anything, her current history in Buck County piled on fresh pain, and now she could add confusion to the mix. What *was* she going to do?

She needed to talk to Rylan. Tell him everything about the worst day of her life. She owed him that much. Then she would ask him for help regarding Noah. If the innocent little fellow had no decent family willing to take him in, Erin would fight tooth and nail to ensure Noah remained with her. Surely, the sheriff would fight for that result alongside her.

With weariness dragging his feet like weights, Rylan walked across the parking lot of the chain hotel in Drover's Creek where Erin and Noah had taken refuge. Stars spangled the blue-black night sky in a glittering dome over the sage-crusted earth, but tonight he had no heart to appreciate the stark magnificence that was unique to desert environments. A few hours ago, Erin had called to say she needed to talk to him as soon as possible and would wait up until he was free to stop by.

Annie had offered Erin and Noah her home as a haven once more, but Erin had declined, stating she'd put the woman out enough. The action felt like pulling away. Like leaving.

What had he expected? Rylan jerked open the hotel's front door with more force than he'd intended and strode into the lobby and up the stairs to the second floor. With the return of her memories, Erin had been able to make a phone call to her bank, report her debit card stolen and request some cash to tide her over. She was independent again, and he was glad for her. Not so glad for himself and what that might mean to his chances of keeping her in his life.

Rylan knocked on the door to Erin's room. His heart leaped as she called out, asking who was there. He loved her voice. He loved everything about her, but he couldn't tell her that. He'd never respect himself if he manipulated her in any way to remain in Drover's Creek.

At his reply, Erin opened the door and stood, gazing

up at him. No smile. Rylan's gut clenched as she motioned for him to enter. He stepped inside to find Noah seated on a blanket on the floor, playing with toys. At least he got a grin from the little guy, who quickly went back to gnawing at a teething rattle.

"Please, sit down," Erin said in a formal tone and gestured at the desk chair.

Rylan's stomach clenched, but he put on a stoic face. "Maybe you'll want to see this first." He pulled a folded piece of paper from his shirt pocket.

Gingerly, she took it from him and held it between her thumb and forefinger. "What is it?"

"I got in touch with the district court judge, and he's issued an injunction to allow you to retain temporary custody of Noah under Family Services supervision until and unless a suitable family member is located, at which time your custody would be terminated. Or until and unless you undergo the vetting process to become a foster parent or to adopt, in which case, your custody would become permanent."

The smile he'd hoped for beamed full wattage from her face. "Thank you!"

She rushed forward and threw her arms around him. He tentatively returned the hug, not trusting himself to commit to the embrace. He'd never be able to let her go.

Erin pulled away from him with a return to sobriety and again motioned for him to have a seat. He complied, and she took up a perch on the edge of the easy chair in the corner.

"I want to tell you about my husband and my baby. Maybe then you'll understand my decision about what to do next."

"You don't have to revisit painful mem—"

She forestalled his words with a lifted hand. "No, I do." The muscles in her throat clenched, and then she let out a gust of air. "Dirck was a medic in the Royal Canadian Navy. He was killed during a rescue mission in international waters. I was told he gave his life to save others."

Her gaze dropped to her lap, and she rubbed her palms up and down on her jeans-clad legs. "But his wasn't the only life sacrificed. During the last trimester of my pregnancy, I developed a condition called placental abruption, which means the placenta partially separated from my uterus, potentially decreasing nutrients to the baby and risking my life from sudden bleeding. My ob-gyn ordered me to bed, but the news of my husband's death brought on premature labor and full separation of the placenta. I was rushed into surgery, and the baby was taken via cesarean section, but it was too late. My little Cara didn't make it, and I nearly died, as well For a long time afterward, a part of me wished I had joined my husband and daughter. The job in Idaho is to give me a fresh start, far away from the site of all those painful memories."

By the time her story concluded, Erin's voice had grown hoarse and wetness coated her cheeks. The sting in Rylan's eyes overflowed into a tear tracking into the corner of his mouth. The salty tang settled on his tongue.

Erin wavered a smile at him. "Thank you for crying with me."

Rylan wiped his cheek with a rough hand and swallowed against a full throat. "You're welcome."

Conversation lapsed. Their deep breathing in and out, nearly in unison, and Noah's baby gurgles supplied the only sounds in the room.

"You said the job in Idaho *is* to give you a fresh start." Rylan broke the near silence. "You're still going?"

"I am."

A fist closed around Rylan's heart, but he forced his expression to remain neutral. "I understand."

"I made a commitment," she said. "I've got to give it a shot. I'm still grieving. I need time to process everything that happened here, too." Her words came out in a tumbling rush, then abruptly halted. "I'm sorry," she added a few seconds later.

"You have nothing to be sorry for." He rose. "You behaved with bravery and distinction in a horrible and hazardous situation. Your husband would have been proud."

Erin rose also. "I appreciate your perspective on that more than you know. I'll probably see you at the trials for Spencer and his people." Her eyes still sparkled with moisture that hadn't yet become tears.

Rylan headed for the door on robotic legs. "I wish you and Noah well."

He supposed he should add *goodbye*, but he couldn't choke out the word.

SEVENTEEN

Nine months later

Erin drove into the small Wyoming town from the same direction she'd left Drover's Creek all those months ago—west. She cruised past the tiny mom-and-pop motel, with its adjoining cabins, where she'd served as bait for would-be killers. Not the tiniest shudder ran through her. She was proud of that day and the others surrounding it, for everything she and the law enforcement community and the people of the town had done to provide for her and Noah and keep them safe. Much of the county had turned out for a going-away party for her and the baby a week after the harrowing events had concluded, and she was no longer needed for statements and interviews.

Then she and Noah had left for Boise nine months ago, but this was not the first time she'd been back to Buck County. She'd had to testify in the trials of the two individuals who attacked her in the motel, as well as the outlaw biker who had assaulted her in Annie's home. The community had greeted her and made over Noah like they were long-lost cousins, cementing even further the place Drover's Creek had claimed in her heart. The trials for the other offenders had taken place at the Wyoming District Court in Casper. Each occasion had brought her together with Sheriff Rylan Pierce, and every encounter deepened her attraction for him. They'd enjoyed meals out together, and Erin had struggled not to consider them dates.

Maybe it was time she let go of the past and embraced the future—provided he felt the same way. She thought so, hoped so, but... Well, she had a good excuse for the visit, anyway. Her joyful news was cause for celebration, and there was no one she'd rather celebrate with—correction, no *group* of people she'd rather celebrate with. Including one special individual in the mix.

Erin pulled into a parking spot outside the law enforcement headquarters building. Nothing had changed about the redbrick facade or the neighborhood. Barb's Café across the street looked to be doing a brisk business, as usual. Maybe the cop crowd could add to it if everyone got as excited as she was about her announcement and wanted to grab a meal together.

Still, she held back from climbing out of the vehicle and heading inside. What if the sheriff was out on a call or too busy to see her? Erin tucked her lower lip between her teeth and nibbled. Until this moment, with her stomach going all queasy, she hadn't realized how much she needed her surprise visit to go perfectly. She had no doubt her news would be received enthusiastically, but she needed something more—a sign from a certain someone that a life change she was considering would mesh with another person's fervent wishes.

"Get a grip, girl," she told herself out loud. "And trust

God. He's got this and knows what's best for people."
For a long time after her grievous personal losses, Erin
had lost sight of that fact, but now her faith had been
restored stronger than ever. "Isn't that right, Noah?"

Erin turned her head to look into the back seat. The
fifteen-month-old gazed back at her from his big-boy
car seat, the infant carrier months in the past. The fake
birthmark on his tummy was also long in the past. The
government had found and confiscated the sizable contents of the bitcoin wallet, but they'd awarded Noah a
not-inconsiderable finder's fee, so to speak. Erin had
made sure the money sat in an account earmarked as the
little boy's college fund. Noah could attend any school
he wanted, for however long he wanted, and not owe a
dime when he finished. Or, if he preferred a more vo-
cational route for his future, the money would set him
up in business. In the meantime, Erin cherished guid-
ing Noah through every step of his growing-up process.

Speaking of the growing-up process, she got out of
the car and released the little boy from his buckles, then
set him on his feet, her hand in his. He walked beside
her and tackled the big step up the curb and onto the
sidewalk with hardly a hitch in his stride. Honestly, it
seemed like he'd gone from crawling to running in a
matter of days as soon as he hit eleven months old. The
kid hadn't slowed down since—as he demonstrated by
tugging Erin toward the doors of the law enforcement
offices. Even though he hadn't been here in a while,
he apparently associated the place with attention and
treats from a whole variety of people who were always
happy to see him.

Would the sheriff be happy to see them? To see *her*?

Squaring her shoulders, Erin opened the door and stepped into the cool interior. It was only May, but the weather had already turned warm in Buck County. At the sound of the bell over the door, Annie looked up from her station, and the woman's full-moon face suddenly beamed like the sun.

"Well, look who's come to visit." She rose from her seat and a buzz-click combination signaled the safety door unlocking between the lobby area and her secure station. "Get on in here, you two! I need hugs."

Thus the welcome began with embraces from all, including Big Dave, who wrapped them both together in his wide arms when they reached his office. Questions peppered the air from multiple directions.

"How's the job going?"

"Have you been well?"

"What's new?"

And exclamations like, "Look how big Noah's gotten!"

The answer to the only question that mattered to Erin wasn't apparent. Where was the sheriff?

"Don't worry, honey." Annie, standing beside her in the bullpen, placed a hand on her arm. "He'll be back any second."

"Am I that obvious?"

The woman snorted. "If you weren't, I'd be worried about you. That man is a prize. Um-hmm. You just go on into his office and wait for him. We won't say a word about you bein' here." She placed a finger to her lips and shooed the two of them into the familiar room.

The space hadn't changed much—not at all, actually. The same slightly battered desk chair, scarred but neatly kept desk with a teetering stack of folders on the corner and the same well-used sofa. Comfortable. Erin was about to settle onto the sofa and scoop Noah onto her lap so the curious toddler wouldn't get into things when familiar footsteps sounded in the bullpen.

"Why is everyone grinning like cats in the milk house?"

At Rylan's voice, Erin's heart skipped a beat.

"Oh, nothing." Annie sniffed. "I'd better get back to my workstation, where staff can call in and keep me *fully apprised* of everything going on with our law enforcement team."

"Now, Annie, I've told you a hundred times—" the voice drew closer to the office doorway "—I didn't tell you Erin and Noah were with me that day because I didn't trust the privacy of our communi—" the sheriff stepped into view "—cations." He finished the word in a faint tone.

Erin's pulse sped up. Did she dare believe what she read on his face? Joy...delight...love?

Rylan couldn't speak because his heart was too busy trying to crowd into his throat. Sure, he'd seen Erin and Noah different times since she'd left town, and they'd communicated via email and text, but the two of them had never simply dropped by. What did the surprise visit mean? He didn't know, so he collected himself and asked.

"I have a big announcement to make," she said, with that smile that always turned him into silly putty. "I was waiting for you to show up so everyone could hear it at the same time."

She picked up Noah, then grabbed Rylan's sleeve and pulled him back out into the squad room.

"Everyone? Annie, too!" she called, and the woman showed herself in the doorway to her station. "It's official! The adoption went through. I'm Noah's mama now."

"Mama," Noah parroted and clapped his hands.

The room erupted in a chorus of laughter and congratulations. Rylan simply stood, grinning and drinking in the sight of Erin and Noah.

"Can you stay long enough for a celebration dinner?" he finally managed to choke out.

Erin's expression sobered, and she met his eyes. An odd mixture of expressions paraded across her face. Fear? Hope? Determination?

"Three months from now, I can stay as long as you'd like me to stay. My contract runs out in Boise, and I might be looking to relocate."

Dense silence fell over the room. The oxygen seemed to vacate Rylan's lungs. Someone poked him in the back. He could guess who without looking behind him.

"Buck County could use your services." He somehow managed not to stutter. "But I doubt we can offer you the compensation package of a large city."

His face heated. *What a tactless thing to say.* Not at all what he *wanted* to say.

A soft smile appeared on Erin's face like she agreed with his assessment but was willing to overlook the clumsiness.

"There are other attractions to Buck County." The smile widened.

Did she mean what he hoped she meant?

Another poke in the back. "Kiss her, you big lummox."

So he did.

EPILOGUE

Six months later

"You may kiss the bride," Pastor Waltz said.

So Rylan did. The warmth and welcome of the lips pressed against his were as wonderful as the first time. Then he turned with his new wife to face the applause of the beaming audience. A lot like the first time they kissed in his office, too. Everyone he—no, *they*—cared about was there for them.

He gazed at his wife, and she gazed back at him. *I love you*, they mouthed at each other.

"Daddy!" a childish voice cried out, and a sturdy little body dressed in a miniature tuxedo collided with his legs.

Laughing, Rylan scooped Noah up in one arm. He linked the other with his bride, and together the three of them walked up the aisle. A newly-formed family on their way to making a good life full of faith and love together.

* * * * *

Dear Reader,

I'm delighted you joined me on this journey of self-discovery and healing for both Emily/Erin and Rylan. I hope you found satisfaction in their story. Danger brought them close, but love kept them together and trumped the grief in both of their lives.

Grief and loss are facts of our earthly existence. Everyone is, at some level, struggling to deal with these feelings and the occurrences that caused them. I don't know what I would do without God's constant presence in my life to sustain me through pain. God's faithful and unchanging love provides an anchor while we pass through the coping and healing journey that is rarely straightforward and always unique to our personalities and situations.

When dealing with raw emotions, pat solutions sound trite, and I don't mean to suggest anything rote or canned in my characters' journeys. However, I do hope something about their struggles and victories touched your heart and you came away from the story enriched or comforted.

Thank you again for reading this book. I enjoy hearing from my readers and can be reached at jnelson@jillelizabethnelson.com. Information about my other books can be found at www.jillelizabethnelson.com.

In His Love,
Jill

Get 3 FREE REWARDS!

We'll send you 2 FREE Books plus a FREE Mystery Gift.

FREE
Value Over
$20

Both the **Love Inspired®** and **Love Inspired® Suspense** series feature compelling novels filled with inspirational romance, faith, forgiveness and hope.

YES! Please send me 2 FREE novels from the Love Inspired or Love Inspired Suspense series and my FREE gift (gift is worth about $10 retail). After receiving them, if I don't wish to receive any more books, I can return the shipping statement marked "cancel." If I don't cancel, I will receive 6 brand-new Love Inspired Larger-Print books or Love Inspired Suspense Larger-Print books every month and be billed just $6.49 each in the U.S. or $6.74 each in Canada. That is a savings of at least 16% off the cover price. It's quite a bargain! Shipping and handling is just 50¢ per book in the U.S. and $1.25 per book in Canada.* I understand that accepting the 2 free books and gift places me under no obligation to buy anything. I can always return a shipment and cancel at any time by calling the number below. The free books and gift are mine to keep no matter what I decide.

Choose one: ☐ **Love Inspired**   ☐ **Love Inspired**   ☐ **Or Try Both!**
                Larger-Print   **Suspense**   (122/322 & 107/307
                (122/322 BPA GRPA)   **Larger-Print**   BPA GRRP)
                                            (107/307 BPA GRPA)

Name (please print)

Address   Apt. #

City   State/Province   Zip/Postal Code

Email: Please check this box ☐ if you would like to receive newsletters and promotional emails from Harlequin Enterprises ULC and its affiliates. You can unsubscribe anytime.

Mail to the **Harlequin Reader Service:**
IN U.S.A.: P.O. Box 1341, Buffalo, NY 14240-8531
IN CANADA: P.O. Box 603, Fort Erie, Ontario L2A 5X3

Want to try 2 free books from another series! Call 1-800-873-8635 or visit www.ReaderService.com.

---

*Terms and prices subject to change without notice. Prices do not include sales taxes, which will be charged (if applicable) based on your state or country of residence. Canadian residents will be charged applicable taxes. Offer not valid in Quebec. This offer is limited to one order per household. Books received may not be as shown. Not valid for current subscribers to the Love Inspired or Love Inspired Suspense series. All orders subject to approval. Credit or debit balances in a customer's account(s) may be offset by any other outstanding balance owed by or to the customer. Please allow 4 to 6 weeks for delivery. Offer available while quantities last.

Your Privacy—Your information is being collected by Harlequin Enterprises ULC, operating as Harlequin Reader Service. For a complete summary of the information we collect, how we use this information and to whom it is disclosed, please visit our privacy notice located at corporate.harlequin.com/privacy-notice. From time to time we may also exchange your personal information with reputable third parties. If you wish to opt out of this sharing of your personal information, please visit readerservice.com/consumerchoice or call 1-800-873-8635. **Notice to California Residents**—Under California law, you have specific rights to control and access your data. For more information on these rights and how to exercise them, visit corporate.harlequin.com/california-privacy.

LIRLIS23

HARLEQUIN
PLUS

Try the best multimedia subscription service for romance readers like you!

Read, Watch and Play.

Experience the easiest way to get the romance content you crave.

Start your **FREE TRIAL** at
www.harlequinplus.com/freetrial: